SPECIAL MESSAGE TO READERS

THE ULVERSCROFT FOUNDATION
(registered UK charity number 264873)
was established in 1972 to provide funds for research, diagnosis and treatment of eye diseases. Examples of major projects funded by the Ulverscroft Foundation are:-

- The Children's Eye Unit at Moorfields Eye Hospital, London
- The Ulverscroft Children's Eye Unit at Great Ormond Street Hospital for Sick Children
- Funding research into eye diseases and treatment at the Department of Ophthalmology, University of Leicester
- The Ulverscroft Vision Research Group, Institute of Child Health
- Twin operating theatres at the Western Ophthalmic Hospital, London
- The Chair of Ophthalmology at the Royal Australian College of Ophthalmologists

You can help further the work of the Foundation by making a donation or leaving a legacy. Every contribution is gratefully received. If you would like to help support the Foundation or require further information, please contact:

THE ULVERSCROFT FOUNDATION
The Green, Bradgate Road, Anstey
Leicester LE7 7FU, England
Tel: (0116) 236 4325
website: www.foundation.ulverscroft.com

THE DARK BOATMAN

Five chilling tales: a family's history is traced back for four centuries — with no instance of a death recorded . . . The tale of an aunt who wanders out to the graveyard each night . . . A manor house is built on cursed land, perpetuating the evil started there long ago . . . The fate of a doctor, investigating the ravings of a man sent mad by the things he has witnessed . . . The evil residing at Dark Point lighthouse where the Devil himself was called up . . .

Books by John Glasby
in the Linford Mystery Library:

THE SAVAGE CITY
A TIME FOR MURDER
DEATH NEVER STRIKES TWICE
THE DARK DESTROYER
DARK CONFLICT
THE UNDEAD
DEATH COMES CALLING
MURDER IS MY SHADOW
DARK LEGION
THE WHEEL SPINS THIRTEEN
MYSTERY OF THE CRATER
ROSES FOR A LADY
PROJECT JOVE
THE MISSING HEIRESS MURDERS

JOHN GLASBY

THE DARK BOATMAN

Complete and Unabridged

LINFORD
Leicester

First published in Great Britain

First Linford Edition
published 2013

A catalogue record for this book is available from the British Library.

ISBN 978–1–4448–1653–2

Published by
F. A. Thorpe (Publishing)
Anstey, Leicestershire

Set by Words & Graphics Ltd.
Anstey, Leicestershire
Printed and bound in Great Britain by
T. J. International Ltd., Padstow, Cornwall

This book is printed on acid-free paper

1

The Dark Boatman

When I received a letter from my late uncle's solicitors informing me that, as the last of the family line, I had been left the old mansion overlooking the sea on the south coast of Cornwall, my first instinctive impulse was to ask them to advertise the place for immediate sale since I had no wish to cut myself off completely in such an isolated spot. I had visited my uncle on only one occasion in my lifetime, more than fifteen years before, and my memories of that visit were far from pleasant.

I was seventeen at the time and it had been late autumn with low cloud and an eternal mist sweeping in from the sea, making it impossible to see anything of the surrounding countryside. I had been a virtual prisoner within the ancient house for two whole weeks and my uncle, who lived the life of a recluse, shunning all contact with the few neighbours he had, was not a fit companion for a youth. He had spent all of the day and most of the night poring over musty old tomes in the library which, though well-stocked with volumes, held only queer literature concerning myths and histories of races no more recent than the ancient Greeks.

The mansion itself had a history almost as long. Parts of it dated back to the time of the second William and the more modern renovations were in the Gothic style, with long, gloomy corridors and narrow passages which intersected in such puzzling patterns that it was easy to lose one's way in the labyrinthine maze which extended from one wing to the other.

Two things, however, conspired to force me to change my mind and move from my native Yorkshire to Cornwall. The first was my health, which had been deteriorating somewhat over the past four years. My doctor was of the considered opinion that the salubrious nature of the Cornish weather would be more conducive to a return to better health than the wind-swept moors of Yorkshire. With summer approaching, the warmer climate would undoubtedly prove both beneficial and invigorating.

The second reason was a further letter, which arrived six days after the first. Like the other, it came from my uncle's solicitors, but inside was a second envelope with my name on it written in my uncle's spidery script in the India ink I remembered him using.

'My dear nephew,' he wrote. 'By the time you receive this I will have departed this earth and as you are my only heir, there are certain points I must bring to your notice concerning the family mansion at Tormouth. These may appear strange to one unaccustomed to our ways but I earnestly assure you they are not the product of a senile or deranged mind and must be followed implicitly. The duty of carrying them out now falls upon you and if it is of any consolation to you, as the only living Dexter, yours will be the final act in the tradition of the Dexters that has been carried on for more centuries than you would ever believe. You will find the key you seek in the concealed compartment of my desk. The opener is the left arabesque. *But use it not until the time is right unless you call over Him who comes only at the appointed hour.* And how shall you know the time? That is given by the clock in the upper room. I adjure you to watch it closely for no one knows the hour when the key must be used.'

I read this strange letter several times, unable to make either head or tail of it. I was well aware I was the last in a long line of Dexters, that I could trace my lineage back, unbroken, for more than eighteen hundred years. But what was all this rigmarole about a key? A key to which lock? And as for keeping continuous watch on a certain clock, waiting for some particular preordained hour to strike — that made no sense to me at all. Nonetheless, the contents of the letter wetted my natural curiosity and I knew that, whatever happened, I had to move into that ancient manor if only to satisfy myself as to the real reason behind my uncle having written such a bizarre epistle.

I did not, however, intend to go alone; at least not until I had discovered all I could about the place and its curious secrets. I decided to ask a colleague of mine, Michael Ambrose, to accompany me. I knew him for a gifted antiquarian, well versed in ancient history and many of the old myths and religions. When I approached him, he accepted with alacrity for he had read a great deal about my family history and the strange stories that surrounded the mansion on the cliffs.

Accordingly, we both took the express to Penzance, arriving early in the evening on a glorious late spring day. My recollection of Tormouth was vague and prone to the inevitable inaccuracies associated with a brief memory of more than fifteen years before. However, we soon discovered there was no public transport which would take us there even at that early hour of the evening. There was, we learned, a bus that went out to Tormouth the next morning although it might be possible to hire a car for our purpose.

Since we were both anxious to reach the mansion as quickly as possible we decided on the latter course and obtained directions to the nearest garage where we might obtain such transport.

The garage proprietor seemed willing to hire us a car, several of which were available. But his demeanour changed dramatically when we mentioned our destination. Now he became oddly reluctant, maintaining that Tormouth was a place with an evil reputation, one that stretched back for more years than he could remember. No one knew for certain just what it was about the place that instilled such weird notions into people's minds but it was a tangible thing best not ignored.

I forbore to tell him my name for I had the feeling that much of the outside animosity and superstitious fear directed towards the village was primarily against my family and mention of the name Dexter might be more than enough to make him refuse point-blank to provide us with a car.

In the end, after much forcible argument, he agreed to let us have a decrepit vehicle, which, from its very appearance, did not look capable of taking us to our destination. However, since beggars could not be choosers we were forced to accept his offer with as much grace as we could muster.

Half an hour later, we left Penzance and took the road east, following the directions we had been given. Dusk had already settled over the countryside and we drove in silence for almost half an hour, entering terrain that grew more barren and wild with every passing mile. Gripping the wheel, I peered intently through the dusty windscreen, searching for some sign of the signpost we had been told to watch out for. Several narrow tracks led off the road but none of these were signposted and were little more than rutted paths leading apparently nowhere across deserted moorland and low, rounded hills that brooded oppressively on the skyline.

Then Ambrose suddenly called my

attention to something lying half-hidden in the ditch by the side of the road. I immediately stopped the car and we both got out to examine it. It was an ancient battered signpost which had once been pointed off to the left for there, less than five yards from where we stood, a track, somewhat wider than the others we had seen earlier, snaked towards the distant horizon. Ambrose went down on one knee and I heard his grunt of astonishment. The sign bore the legend *Tormouth — 5 miles* in faded letters and I thought this was what he had seen.

Then I looked to where he was pointing and saw the wooden post had not fallen through decay due to long years of standing in all sorts of weather. It had been deliberately axed through the base. Whether local inhabitants had committed this act to erase all reference to Tormouth, or the villagers themselves had done it to preserve their isolation, we could not tell. But as we got back into the car we were both oddly disturbed by what we had found. Clearly, the garage proprietor had not exaggerated when he had spoken of the evil reputation Tormouth possessed.

We turned off the road with a growing sense of trepidation. Now the surrounding countryside grew more sinister and somber in its overall aspect. The car lurched and slid over numerous potholes and in places the thick, thorny branches slashed and tore at the vehicle on both sides.

At times, the overgrown bushes assumed grotesque shadows in the approaching darkness and I was forced to switch on the headlights in order to see the way for there were many twists and turns ahead and obstacles became more numerous so that avoiding action had to be taken quickly and decisively.

We had not been more than two miles along the track when the mass of dark, ominous cloud we had noticed earlier swept down on us and it began to rain. Had it been possible to turn I might have considered returning to Penzance and setting out again in the morning for driving had now become extremely difficult. But it was all I could do to keep the car on the road, which was now rapidly worsening because of the rain. The aged wipers did little to keep the windscreen clear and we were soon splashing through deepening puddles that stretched clear across the road.

Then we crested a high hill and down below us, just visible, was the sea and off to our right we made out a tiny cluster of dim lights, which told us we were approaching our destination. Now the smell of the sea was strong in our nostrils. Curiously, the state of the road improved. At some time, it had been surfaced and the reason for this improvement soon became evident. Less than half a mile further on, the ground on our right dropped away steeply towards the rocky beach.

In spite of the relatively new road surface I had to drive carefully now. The rough gravel was wet and slippery and one wrong move could send us crashing over the cliff onto the waiting rocks below. In addition, the headlights were not powerful enough to penetrate far into the teeming rain.

Finally, however, we headed down into the village and stopped halfway along the cobbled street. The place seemed utterly deserted. An air of abandonment lay over the low-roofed houses and crumbling stone jetty that thrust like a long tongue into the sea. The tide was out and a mile or so offshore I could just make out twin pinnacles of black rock which stood up from the ocean like two mighty guardians offering a safe entry into the tiny harbour.

Fortunately, I had no need to ask directions of any of the inhabitants. I well remembered the obvious dislike these folk had of my uncle and did not doubt this animosity would also be extended towards anyone of the hated name of Dexter. From what I could recall there were many in the village who had regarded him as some kind of wizard and although such a notion might have been laughed at by townsfolk, here such beliefs had always been strongly held.

I started the car again and drove slowly past the shuttered windows fronting the street. At the end of the village there was a narrow road, which led in a series of tortuous bends to the mansion, which we were soon able to pick out as a gaunt, black silhouette against the skyline.

The rain was still coming down in torrents as we drove through the tall metal gates and along the drive between huge oaks and elms, swinging around in front of the house.

No lights showed in any of the windows. Overhead, tall Gothic turrets and spires showed against the dark sky. I heard Ambrose gasp as he caught sight of it for the first time, looming before us in a great spectral mass of age-old stone.

I could guess at his feelings; I had felt them myself fifteen years before. As I have said earlier, my forebears had made various alterations to the original structure over the centuries resulting in an oddly clashing conglomeration of architectural styles that had certainly not enhanced the overall appearance in any way. Indeed, the only softening effect came from the thick layers of ivy along the walls, for time and weather had had the opposite effect; making the angular abutments and towers even harsher and starker in their general outline.

We left the car parked in front of the main door and hurriedly transferred our few belongings onto the porch where I selected the correct key from the bunch I had received from the solicitors and threw open the door. Inside, we found a couple of lamps for there was no electricity and in the yellow glow explored the nearer regions. The interior did not appear to have changed at all since my one and only previous visit. Apart from a thin layer of whitish dust, which covered everything, the place was just as my uncle had left it.

The wide hallway with the wide staircase leading off ground level at the far end and the huge oak table in the middle of the stone floor, chairs arranged round the walls, the broad open fireplace and the few pieces of bric-a-brac my uncle had collected over the years; all blended into a familiar scene which struck me with the force of a physical blow, bringing back recollections of my unforgettable experiences one and a half decades earlier.

An hour later, we had made ourselves

reasonably comfortable. There were four bedrooms on the ground floor in the West Wing and Ambrose and I had chosen a couple of these for ourselves. There was clearly a lot to be done before the place was fit to be lived in but that would have to wait. Now that I had inherited the mansion and was master there I intended to see that changes were made. Structurally, the building was very sound but the interior was in urgent need of complete renovation and modernisation.

We were both tired now. After eating a brief meal of cold meat that we had brought with us, we retired to our rooms. But weary as I was, I found it difficult to sleep. There was something odd about the place, which I could not define. I was well aware that all old houses possess curious atmospheres which can be sensed strongly, particularly by those sensitive to such auras and there were also my own remembrances of this place, which I had never thought to visit again. But it was something more than this; as if my uncle had never left this house but some part of him still remained to ensure that I carried out those peculiar instructions he had outlined in his letter.

When, at length, I did fall into an uneasy doze it was to be assailed by troubled dreams in which I seemed to be standing in some great subterranean cavern where a vast, thunderous cataract plunged into a bottomless abyss and in the foreground, on a rocky ledge, stood my uncle pointing an admonishing finger at me and shouting words which I could not hear above the endless roar of the water falling into the terrifying chasm.

When I woke it was grey dawn and I was sweating profusely. I threw off the coverlet and dressed hurriedly, feeling an unaccustomed chill on my body. Ambrose was awake and had lit a fire in the hearth.

Over breakfast, Ambrose plied me with questions concerning my immediate plans. I had to confess that so far, I had given but scant thought to them, waiting to see what state the house was in before deciding what needed to be done and in what order things could reasonably be carried out. After some discussion, we decided to drive into

Penzance that morning where I wished to visit my late uncle's solicitors and Ambrose would approach various architects with a view to one coming out to Tormouth to look over the place and draw up plans for its modernisation. Ambrose would also purchase provisions, sufficient to last us for some time for I doubted if we would be able to obtain any in the village.

The weather had turned fine and sunny once more as we drove through Tormouth and we were acutely aware of the sullen glances of the few people abroad on the street. But our spirits rose a little as we left the sea behind and progressed across the bare moorland. By the time we arrived in Penzance the sun was hot and there was not a cloud in the sky.

Leaving Ambrose, I searched out the offices of Poulton and Forsythe, the solicitors, where I was shown into the office of Andrew Forsythe, a small, balding man in his late fifties who received me courteously and ushered me to a chair. Even though he had probably been expecting me to call sometime, it seemed my presence there made him distinctly uneasy.

'I trust you received the letter your uncle wrote just before he . . . died,' he said, placing the tips of his fingers together and staring at me over the fleshy pyramid.

I assured him I had and mentioned the strange contents.

'I'm afraid I can't enlighten you on that subject. To be quite honest, I had very little to do with your uncle. He was, as you know, a man of, shall we say — peculiar, habits. He had no visitors I know of, staying quite alone in that house on the cliffs. I think I should also warn you that the inhabitants of the village will not take too kindly to your arrival. They're a clannish and highly supersti-tious lot and unfortunately this is no recent thing.'

I must have looked at him in surprise, for he went on hurriedly: 'From the records which are still extant, the Dexters have lived there for nearly a thousand years and wild rumours concerning them have circulated throughout the surrounding countryside for almost as long as that.'

'What sort of rumours?' I asked. Forsythe's expression had given me pause.

'Oh, the usual kind of thing one comes across in isolated communities such as this.' Forsythe tried to appear offhand about the subject, but this was belied by the look of gravity on his face. 'The family was suspected of sorcery during the Middle Ages but, curiously, no action seems to have been taken against them in spite of the infamous witchcraft trials, which took place elsewhere.'

The news did not surprise me. My family had always kept itself to itself and it was inevitable that, in such circumstances, such suspicions should be levelled against them. When Forsythe made no move to embellish his remarks, I changed the subject.

'Now that I've taken over the house and property there are a number of changes I wish to make. I trust there are no legal reasons why I should not do so.'

'None of which I am aware,' he assured me. 'Indeed, from what little I've seen of the house, it has always struck me that the lack of modern amenities is something which should be rectified as soon as possible.'

'Then I shall do that without delay,' I told him.

He nodded in acquiescence. 'I consider that to be a wise move,' he said.

After a pause, I got up to take my leave of him but, as I did so, another thought struck me, born of the sudden recollection of how he had paused oddly when he had mentioned my uncle's death.

'I wonder if you could tell me where my uncle is buried. I'd like to see the grave.'

The look he gave me at that moment sent a strange feeling of apprehension through me. For several seconds, he seemed to have difficulty in answering me. It was evident my question had somehow disconcerted him.

Finally, he said harshly, 'I'm afraid I'm not in a position to do that, Mr. Dexter.'

'Why not?' I asked indignantly. 'Surely

he must have been buried somewhere. There was no reference to him having been cremated.'

'The point is I've no information as to where he was buried. I merely received the news that he had died and the estate was to pass to you as his only living relative.'

'Do you know if there is a family vault?' It had suddenly occurred to me that this was the only possible answer. 'And, if so, who carried out the ceremony?'

'I presume there must be one somewhere, but as to its whereabouts I'm afraid I'm totally ignorant.'

I was utterly astonished and made no attempt to hide it. 'Then how can you be so sure he's dead?'

'Oh, there's no doubt about that.' He spoke with an enforced calmness in an attempt to quieten my ruffled composure. I also got the impression he would not welcome any further questions on this particular subject. That there was a mystery here I did not doubt. But it was equally obvious I would gain little, or no, further information from him.

I decided I would have to make further, and more detailed, enquiries. My first attempts ended in failure. I ascertained the names and addresses of all the undertakers in Penzance and visited each in turn enquiring about my uncle but the response was the same in every case. There had been no interment at Tormouth and my uncle's name was not known to any of them.

I then sought out the offices of the *Penzance Gazette* where, after some deliberation, the editor gave permission for me to peruse the back copies of the newspaper. I soon came across a small notice detailing the death of my uncle but apart from the name, address and date, there were no additional details given in the brief insertion. It was all very strange; almost as though, apart from this brief reference, he had never existed.

My last call, before meeting Ambrose at the car, was to the main library where I spent an hour perusing the old records pertaining to Tormouth. Here I came across several references to the Dexter family. These were, in the main, quite ordinary with but one hint of the bizarre. The documents traced the history of the Dexter family back for almost four centuries. In most cases, records were given of births and marriages in the family, *but there was not a single instance of a death recorded!*

I was now beset by the nagging suspicion that if there was any logic behind my discoveries, I could not find it. Those strange instructions given by my uncle, coupled with these oddly disturbing facts, made me wonder if I had done the right thing in coming here and taking up residence in the mansion. Could there possibly be any truth in those spectral tales that had been rife three or four centuries ago? Had there been witches and warlocks in the family who had dabbled in powers more ancient and perhaps more powerful than Christianity?

I found it hard to believe. To the best of my knowledge, such stories were usually put about by superstitious folk, often for the purpose of personal gain or revenge.

When I rejoined Ambrose, I informed him of my findings, remarking how so much of my time and efforts appeared to have been wasted. For his own part, he informed me that he had managed to engage the services of an architect who had promised to come out to the mansion the following day to look over the place and discuss plans with me. He had also purchased sufficient food to last us for at least a couple of weeks.

That afternoon, we located my uncle's desk in the large room at the rear of the building, which he had obviously used as a study. It was a huge piece of furniture, massively constructed in solid wood with numerous drawers containing sheaths of paper, which I laid aside for the time being, intending to go through them closely in case they should yield more information about the family.

The back of the desk was intricately carved with curious designs and motifs, some of which were of an extremely repellent nature. Ambrose had brought a lamp since very little daylight succeeded in penetrating the small windows and he placed this on top of the desk so that we could examine the carvings closely. There was such a confusing intermingling of designs that we had some difficulty determining which arabesque my uncle had referred to in his letter, and it was more by trial and error that I succeeded in finding one which gave slightly as I ran my finger over it.

At first, nothing happened. Then there was a faint click as if some concealed mechanism that had been long unused had suddenly grated into motion. The next moment, a section at the side slid forward, revealing a dark cavity. It was not very large, and I could only get the tips of my fingers inside. Nevertheless, I managed to locate something heavy and metallic which, by dint of careful manoeuvring, I managed to extricate. Holding it up in the lamplight, we saw that it was a large key made out of some yellow metal deeply etched with cryptic symbols, which Ambrose considered to be related to Etruscan. But since no one had yet succeeded in translating this ancient script, it clearly afforded us no information as to their meaning.

There was no accompanying parchment or note of any kind in the drawer and I closed it reluctantly.

'Do you have any idea which lock this key is supposed to fit?' Ambrose asked, eyeing me curiously across the desk.

I shook my head. 'Only what my uncle wrote in his letter that it must not be used until the proper time unless I call forth Him who comes only at the appointed hour.'

'If I were you, I'd throw it into the sea,' Ambrose said earnestly. 'Maybe you'll say I'm being nothing but an old fool, but in my line of work you get a feel about certain objects and that's definitely one of them. There's something evil about it, something horrible. Don't ask me what it is, because I can't tell you. I only know that it's incredibly old and whatever purpose it's been used for, it's something to be shunned like the plague.'

'Now you're being every bit as superstitious as the folk in the village,' I admonished him. 'There's bound to be a door somewhere in the house it fits and I'll find it. My guess is that whatever is in the room will give us the answer to the mystery about this place.'

My companion did not answer. Now he had made his point, he had transferred his attention to the rows of books on the shelves around the study. An examination of these showed that my uncle had possessed a catholic taste in reading. Curiously, they were not arranged, as in most cases, alphabetically by author or title, but chronologically according to their date of publication. There were several dealing with Einstein's theories of relativity, Minkowski's proposals regarding space-time and the block theory of the universe and Cantor's mathematics of transinfinite numbers. As we moved further along the shelves we came across much older volumes and there was a gradual change from science to alchemy and mythology. Most of these were completely unknown to me, but Ambrose recognised some of them which were written in a wide variety of languages; Greek, Latin, archaic German, while there were others in weird hieroglyphical characters which neither of us could understand.

Evidently my uncle had been keenly interested in the religions of many parts of the world; the cults of the Polynesians, of Easter Island, Tibet and the early races of both North and South America. Some of the titles gave an indication of their contents; *The Diablerie Daemonalis,* the *Seven Volumes of Ksar, Zegrembi's Ahrimanes Omnipotae,* the *Book of K'yog* and several others which were in manuscript form, with faded characters in mediaeval English which had obviously been copied from still earlier works.

We spent more than an hour going through these fabulously old tomes and our sense of wonderment grew for clearly they represented one of the most complete records in existence of the folklore and legends of many races stretching back to the very beginnings of the human race, or even beyond for some seemed to tell of races on Earth which pre-dated the generally accepted period in time when Man was assumed to have evolved from some earlier stock.

Certain of the books contained lists of spells, chants and incantations supposedly aimed at making contact with demons and spirits and opening the way between our world and other planes of existence coterminous with our own. These, although not uninteresting, we dismissed as being nothing more than the usual claptrap of superstitious charlatans during the Middle Ages. Whether my uncle had actually believed in any of this was unimportant now. Ambrose, however, was keenly interested in them, for he was convinced that there are forces within the universe about which science knows little or nothing, and the idea that there could exist an infinity of other universes which, at certain points, might intersect, and mingle with our own was by no means ridiculous or unscientific.

By now, the hour was growing late and we reluctantly abandoned any further reading for the day. It was growing dark outside and I realised the day had passed too quickly for me to do a number of things I had intended doing. I wanted to examine the overgrown grounds around the house for any sign of a family mausoleum where the remains of my ancestors were buried for it seemed utterly irrational to suppose that they had merely disappeared without a trace. Common sense told me they had to be interred somewhere close by. Considering their reputation, it was inconceivable they would be buried in the village churchyard.

I had also meant to search for the clock my uncle had mentioned in his letter but, knowing from past experience the maze of corridors and passages within the house, I had no wish to do this except in broad daylight.

Accordingly, we retired to the large front room, stoked the fire and prepared a hot meal, the first decent one we had eaten since arriving at the mansion.

I went to my bed early that night, leaving Ambrose reading by the fire.

The wind had got up during the evening and now it whistled and howled among the branches outside causing other noises within the house, which made it difficult for me to fall asleep.

There was a wooden casement banging incessantly somewhere in one of the upper rooms and at times I made out a faint rushing sound which seemed to emanate from below. Not in the foundations themselves but deeper than that, far down in the bowels of the cliff. This I put down to the sound of the tide coming in with the wind.

Eventually, I fell asleep and once more I dreamed of a vast waterfall crashing and thundering into bottomless depths. In my dream I had assumed the role of a passive observer and for a long time it seemed nothing happened apart from the mighty rush of water, tumbling eternally over the huge curving lip of the precipice. This time, however, details were clearer and sharper than in my previous nightmare.

There was a cloying mist in the foreground, which obscured part of my dreaming vision and gradually I became aware that something was moving through it towards me. It was impossible to distinguish what the object was but it was moving slowly and silently towards the bank of the wide river and I knew instinctively it would ground upon the rocks very close to where I stood.

When I woke, jerking upright in the large bed, perspiration dripping from my forehead into my eyes, it was with the sound of the rushing water still ringing in my ears. I was clutching convulsively at the bedclothes and several frantic seconds passed before I realised that the sound was not a fading echo of my dream. It was real and came from deep below the foundations of the ancient house. As if in confirmation of its actuality, I distinctly felt the house shaking as if caught in the grip of some monstrous earth tremor.

When the sound and shaking failed to abate, I got up, threw on my dressing gown and lit the lamp on the bedside table and, leaving my room quietly in order not to awaken Ambrose, I went to the rear of the house where it overlooked the sea, never stopping to realise that if the cause of the sound and shaking came from far below, there would be no sign of anything out of the ordinary outside.

Somehow, I succeeded in opening one of the windows and, in spite of the chill of the strong wind, I leaned out, peering into the darkness. Indeed, at first, I did see nothing that might account for the peculiar phenomenon. Much of the sound had now ceased and all I could hear was the nearby booming of the surf on the rocks. Directly beneath me, the ivied wall fell sheer to the cliff-top, which then continued in an almost unbroken line for a further three hundred feet to the beach for the house was built right on the edge.

The sky was now clear and there was a moon, just past full to the southeast, and in the pale wash of moonlight, I made out the twin pillars of rock far-off in the water, guarding the entrance to the harbour away to my right. The moon threw a glittering radiance upon the water and as I watched I noticed a strange thing. The long sweep of the waves rolling towards the shore was unbroken in both directions. But between the two columns, the reflection of the moonlight was oddly disturbed, broken and churned as if some seething maelstrom whirled between them.

I thought at first it was some trick of the light, an optical illusion. But the more I stared, the more convinced I became that there was, indeed, something beneath the surface of the ocean which was disturbing it, some powerful submerged current, perhaps, driving along an invisible channel.

How long I stood there, shivering in the cold air, it was impossible to tell. But gradually the swirling transfiguration diminished and the ocean resumed its normal aspect.

Once my initial shock had passed, I returned to my room. It was impossible for me to sleep again. For one thing, I dreaded those weird dreams which now seemed bent on plaguing me each night and secondly, my brain was filled with too many conflicting facts; too many urgent questions demanding answers, for me to relax. I lay wide awake until, hearing Ambrose leave his room just as dawn was breaking, I got up and joined him in the parlour.

I questioned him seriously as to whether he had heard anything strange during the night but he had sat reading until after midnight and had then gone to bed, falling into a deep sleep almost at once and had heard nothing.

The arrival of the architect from Penzance pushed the incidents of the night into the background of my mind. He was a youngish man of Midland stock, having only moved to Cornwall within the past year, and he was not given to over-imaginative speculations concerning the house he examined; nor had he any leanings towards the occult and evidently knew very little of the history of the Dexters.

I accompanied him as he went over the house, making brief notes and sketches on a pad as I explained to him exactly what I wanted. It was as we were returning along the long, gloomy upper corridor that a very curious incident occurred. We had paused to look at the rows of family portraits along either side.

'I notice there's no room left for yours as last of the family,' said the architect, indicating to where my uncle's picture occupied the position at the very end of the wall.

'Most of these portraits have been here for centuries,' I said. 'It seemed unlikely whoever arranged spaces for them could have known how many more would be needed.'

The architect stepped forward and, grasping the bottom of my uncle's picture, tilted it slightly in order for it to hang level. It was as he did so that something small and round fell onto the thick carpet and rolled away into the shadows. I went forward, stooped, and picked it up holding it tightly in my fingers. It was a large golden coin with Greek inscriptions on either side, and a head which I did not recognise. I slipped it into my pocket and then led the way downstairs.

After the architect had gone, promising to proceed with his plans and let me see them as soon as possible so that workmen might be engaged to put them into practice, I showed my find to Ambrose for I had never had any interest in things of that kind.

He took it across to the window and examined it curiously, obviously puzzled by its antiquity and the inscriptions.

Finally, he said, 'I must confess I've never come across anything like this before. It's certainly gold and must be some three thousand years old. But the head is one I don't recognise, nor the design on the other side.'

'Can you make out what it is?'

'I'm not sure. It looks like a boat, rather a primitive design and there are leaves, or perhaps flames, in the background. Do you mind if I keep it for a while? I'd like to have the experts look at it. I'll let you have it back.'

'You may keep it if you wish,' I said. 'It's of no interest to me and I've no idea of its worth.'

'It could be extremely valuable,' he remarked, eyeing me dubiously as if reluctant to accept it.

Had I known of its true meaning and value I would certainly never have let him have it for, unwittingly, by that simple act I had brought doom upon both of us. For Ambrose is gone now, like all the others of my accursed family. Some might say he went in my place and my only consolation is that his fate was not as terrible as mine is likely to be.

That afternoon, we decided to explore the upper rooms for I was now anxious to discover the whereabouts of the clock that had featured so strangely in my uncle's letter. But though we searched every room on the top floor we found no sign of anything even remotely resembling a clock. It might have well gone undiscovered had it not been for Ambrose's sharp eyes later that afternoon.

Disappointed in our efforts to find a clock, he went out into the grounds to look, instead, for the family mausoleum, which I was certain had to be located somewhere within walking distance of the house. Most of the grounds lay to one side of the house and at the front where they stretched in the direction of the narrow track that served as a road. Very little vegetation of any kind grew close to the cliff edge for here there was only a meager covering of soil on top of hard rock. But elsewhere stood a veritable forest of tall trees and bushes, which had long gone untended.

The unnatural growth of vegetation was not due only to years of neglect, however. We came across several places where grotesque plants flourished in such wild profusion we were forced to literally hack our way through them. Long, creeping tendrils as thick as my wrist coiled and intertwined among patches of abnormally large fungi of such garish colours and hideous configurations it was almost impossible to believe they were natural species. Everything we saw seemed *changed* as if the roots which penetrated deep into the soil sucked some blasphemous nourishment from the earth, transforming and mutating them into the shapes they now possessed.

The mausoleum, when we eventually found it, was an unobtrusive, low building, concealed within the trees close to the eastern boundary of the property. Very little of the structure was visible apart from the huge door that sloped backward at the bottom of a short flight of steps leading below ground level.

I had not thought to bring a key with me but, to our surprise, the heavy door was not locked and readily yielded to our efforts.

Ambrose had brought a powerful torch and, stepping inside, he shone the beam around the dark interior. It was considerably larger than we had anticipated from the outside, clearly built many centuries earlier from stone blocks which had survived the years remarkably well.

So this was where the Dexter dead lay interred, I mused as I glanced at the long rows of coffins stacked along the walls. That they were indeed those of my ancestors appeared evident from the state of increasing decay, the further they lay from the door. Those against the far wall had all but crumbled into mouldy heaps of dry dust.

Yet there was still a nagging suspicion at the back of my mind, one that had to be confirmed or stilled forever. Motioning Ambrose to hold the torch steady, I gripped the outer edge of the coffin lid nearest me and slid it aside. Tilting the torch, Ambrose shone the beam directly into the coffin, revealing to our startled gaze that it was empty. In my mind, there was no doubt at all that it had never been occupied. An examination of several others confirmed my suspicions, for inwardly, I had been half-expecting something like this, ever since reading through the old records in the Penzance library.

Whatever had taken place whenever one of my ancestors had died, they had never been buried here nor, it seemed, were their deaths ever recorded anywhere!

Closing the vault behind us, we retraced our steps in silence, mystified by our grim discovery, pondering on any possible explanation for this curious state of affairs.

By some misjudgement of our direction we emerged from the trees, not at the point where we had earlier entered but close to the cliff edge with the surf pounding onto the rocks directly below. Thus it was we approached the house at an angle from the rear and, as I have intimated earlier, Ambrose's keen antiquarian eye noticed an odd peculiarity. He drew my attention to it at once.

At the back of the house, midway between two turrets and obviously forming part of the upper floor, an oblong abutment jutted from the wall, standing out for perhaps ten feet. Although it would have been completely invisible from any other direction, it was obvious from where we stood.

There could be only one answer. Somewhere at the end of the long upper corridor was a concealed room. That it wasn't the most ancient part of the house seemed highly significant.

Now convinced that this had to be the room my uncle had written of, we hurriedly made our way inside and up the wide stairway to the upper floor. Had we not known the room was there, it is extremely unlikely we would ever have found it for the means of opening the concealed door was well hidden among the embossed carving on the wall. It took several minutes of painstaking examination of these carvings before Ambrose uttered a sharp exclamation as his questing fingers depressed a small, insignificant portion of the design.

What hidden mechanism controlled the opening and closing of the door we could not tell for it slid snugly into a narrow cavity in the wall. But from the smooth, silent way it moved I guessed it had been in use on several previous occasions.

The room was small and cramped yet it was just possible for both of us to stand side by side. There were no windows, nor had we really expected to find any. By the torchlight we saw that the room was completely empty except for the object that stood against the far wall. It was indeed the clock mentioned by my uncle yet it presented the most singular appearance for it was totally unlike any I had ever seen.

It was about nine feet tall, roughly oblong in shape, rather like a grandfather clock. Yet there the resemblance ended. It bore a large oval face with but a single pointer and around the circumference were all manner of repulsive figures, interspersed with drawings of the sun and moon and planets. The case was not of wood but some kind of black metal, which did not reflect the light from the torch. And although we carried out a minute and meticulous examination of the entire surface we could discover no means of opening the case to determine what sort of mechanism operated it.

By this time, the most horrifying conclusions were pushing their way into my mind but all without any logic to them. That there had to be some connecting link between all of the weird and seemingly inexplicable facts I had ascertained, seemed obvious. Some concealed thread wove continuously through the twisted fabric of myth, ancient belief and genuine reality. I had the feeling it lay right under my nose but I could not see it.

Ambrose would have remained longer in the room for he was clearly fascinated by the clock. At the time, I thought it was because it represented a challenge to him, defying him to probe its secrets. Now I know better for I think, in retrospect, it was this object that drove him to his final act of destruction and left me to face a hideous end.

I finally persuaded him to leave it for the time being and after closing the door by depressing the same motif, we went downstairs and prepared ourselves a meal.

Over dinner, we attempted to make sense out of the confusing information we had in our possession. Most of our talk, however, centred upon the cabalistic nature of the clock. Ambrose was of the opinion that it, and the key we had found, were the central clues to the entire mystery which seemed to hang over my family and, indeed, over the house itself.

Having seen it for myself, I considered it was something best left alone for I had not liked the look of the characters inscribed around the face and I had the uncanny conviction I knew its purpose yet I had never seen it before, nor even suspected its existence.

'Of one thing I am certain,' Ambrose said, sipping his wine slowly. 'It has the appearance of being ancient Greek in origin judging by some of the characters. But I'm confident it pre-dates the earliest Athenian culture by several thousand years.'

'That's impossible,' I argued. 'For one thing, there were no such time-keeping devices as far back in time as that. And secondly, if we're to believe what my uncle wrote, it still works, although in what fashion I don't know. No driving mechanism could possibly remain in working order for that length of time. It would have rusted and crumbled into dust ages ago.'

'Nevertheless, I'm convinced I'm correct.' Ambrose remained adamant in spite of the incontrovertible truth of my statement.

'Even if you're right,' I went on, 'can you tell me what form of energy has kept it going for so long?'

'There are more forces within the universe then you, or science, can even dream of,' he said enigmatically.

There was clearly no point in arguing with him further and we dropped the subject, turning instead to more mundane matters connected with my plans for the renovation of the house interior until it was almost midnight and the fire in the hearth had dwindled to a heap of faintly glowing embers.

That night, my sleep was unbroken by

dreams for the first time since arriving in the house. Yet when I woke, it was with a sudden start. Something had woken me for it was still pitch black outside the window and I lay for several minutes straining to pick out any untoward sound that might have subconsciously alarmed me.

It is not uncommon for sleepers to be awakened by the abrupt stopping of a clock; by the sudden cessation of sound rather than by a sound itself. Thus, it was with me. Complete and utter silence reigned within the house. But even as I grew aware of the singular fact that there was not the slightest creak or gust of wind to be heard — there did come a sound, one I was loath to identify, and yet knew to be the stirring of rushing water.

I slid off the bed and went out of the room, pulling on my dressing gown.

This time, I meant to awaken Ambrose in order to confirm the existence of that unnatural phenomenon I had witnessed the previous night. I knocked loudly on his door and, when there was no answer, flung it open. In the faint wash of moonlight I saw that his bed was empty and the lamp that he kept on the bedside table was gone. That he had been in bed was obvious from the tumbled bedding.

Where could he have gone this ungodly hour of the morning? The first possibility that came into my mind was that he had gone for a drink of water for we had consumed three bottles of wine at supper. Then I recalled his strange, one might almost say *morbid*, fascination with the clock.

I returned hastily to my room and lit my lamp. Enveloped in the yellow pool of light, I made my way cautiously up the stairs, treading carefully to make no sound. Arriving at the top, I paused to listen. I could hear nothing but that earlier noise, like a huge wave washing up some deep cavern and all of the nightmarish terror I had felt in my dream came sweeping over me anew.

Arriving at the end of the corridor I saw that my supposition had been correct. The secret door stood open, but as I approached, shining the light into the room, I saw he was no longer there. The room was empty except for the monstrous clock, which I knew, even then, told no earthly time.

I was just on the point of leaving when something anomalous about the clock caught my eye. It was just a small thing yet it sent a shiver of dread and foreboding through me. The solitary hand had been pointing straight up when Ambrose and I had examined it only a few hours earlier. Now it had moved and the metal tip rested midway across a grinning skull almost halfway around the oval face!

Fighting back the horror that sent my thoughts spinning into a raving turmoil, I fled along the shadowed corridor as if all the demons of the outer spheres were on my heels, taking the stairs two at a time, oblivious of the very real possibility of falling and breaking my neck at the bottom. Somehow, I had to find my companion for I was sure he was in mortal danger.

By some strange instinct, I knew he was in none of the rooms I had visited with the architect that morning. What presentiment led my steps to the door leading down into the cellar, I shall never know. Perhaps some part of my mind subconsciously associated it with the sound of rushing, roaring water I had heard the night before — and could faintly hear now.

The door was open when I reached it although I had always assumed it to be locked. Holding the lamp high in front of my face, I began the descent of the ancient stone steps. Curiously, they stretched deeper into the foundations for the house than I had imagined possible and long before I came to the bottom, they were encrusted with a glittering nitrous covering which made every step precarious in the extreme.

Now the sound of water was louder and I felt I must be approaching its source. I had tried to rationalise the noise by telling myself that the sea flung itself hard against the base of the cliffs whenever the tide came in and odd echoes and reverberations would distort the sound into what I was hearing. Certainly the sheer size of the cellars, when I reached them, would have accounted for such deep-toned resonances as now clambered through the air all around me.

I shouted Ambrose's name at the top of my voice, straining my vision to pick out any movement in the darkness ahead of me. But there came no answer to my repeated calls and I shuffled forward, taking care where I put my feet for there were numerous obstacles littering the cellar floor. The lamplight threw long shadows ahead of me and picked out tall, rearing columns whose tops I was unable to distinguish.

I had taken less than a dozen shuffling steps when I happened to glance down and saw, a little to my left, a line of footprints in the dust and, just beyond them, a second set of prints, fainter than those nearer to where I stood. The one was clearly quite recent, and I knew they could belong to none other than my companion. As for the other, I could not guess whose they were although they could not have been made more than a few months previously — and that could only mean that my uncle had been down here for some reason.

Confident I was now on the right track, I followed the prints into the darkness, finally coming up against a great stone wall which was clearly the boundary of the foundations.

Set in it was a massive metal door and I saw that both sets of prints led up to it and vanished. In the lock was the metal key covered with the weird hieroglyphs. Evidently, Ambrose had taken it from the desk where I had posted for safekeeping. Somehow, he had guessed at its purpose. There was an iron ring just above the lock and I grasped it firmly with one hand and pulled with all my strength. The door opened reluctantly as if it were seldom used.

I had thought to see darkness before me, perhaps another room abutting onto the cellars. Instead, shock and horror paralysed me, held me rooted there, gripped in a frenzy of hallucinatory delirium. I must now choose words with great care for in that horror-filled moment I saw everything; knew why there were never any records of the deaths of my ancestors, nor any trace of their earthly remains.

I realised, in a cataclysm of superstitious fear, the nature of the *time* measured by that unimaginably old clock whose origins lay in the legend-shrouded aeons of time, marking off the hours remaining to each of the Dexters and — by some terrible quirk of fate — poor Ambrose as well. And most terrible of all, the true identity of that mighty river whose nearer shore lay immediately below the Dexter mansion.

My condition as I stood teetering on the brink of that illimitable cavern was one of indescribable mental tumult. Before me an endless flight of steps lead down to the black swirling waters of the great river that ran into a far distance, towards an unseen cataract where it thundered down into abyssal depths, lit by the lurid glare of hellfires pouring up from below.

All this I saw in a single mind-searing glance. But there was more than that. Would to God I had turned and fled back through those noisome cellars before witnessing the final scene. But see it I did and the unbelievable horror and its implications will haunt me for the remainder of my days.

Far, far below me I made out the diminutive figure of Michael Ambrose standing like a man in a dream on the bank of the river. I tried to call his name but nothing more than a feeble croak emerged from my shaking lips. And then, out of the swirling mist that formed a curtain across the foreground, exactly as I had seen it in my dream, something black appeared, heading for the very spot where he stood.

Gliding to the bank, the ebony boat grounded there and the hooded boatman held out a hand to Ambrose. I saw my former companion hand him something which shone yellow in the dim radiance and knew it to be the curious coin which had fallen from behind my uncle's portrait and which I had unwittingly, given to Ambrose. A coin that had no value in this world but was the tribute paid to Charon in return for ferrying the soul across the Styx!

As Ambrose seated himself in the prow of the boat, the boatman thrust away from the bank and in that same instant raised his head to stare upward in my direction, and as he did so the night-black hood fell away and I glimpsed the grinning skull beneath. In that moment, my nerve broke completely. I was babbling insanely at the top of my voice during my precipitous flight through the cellars and up the nitre-coated steps.

I remember little of reaching the top of the steps and slamming the cellar door shut. My earliest coherent memory is of lying on my bed, shivering and shaking and staring at the brightening dawn light beyond the window.

This then was the curse of the Dexters. Only the long-dead members of that forgotten race, which created that hideous clock in the concealed room upstairs could possibly have told me what will happen next. For soon there will come a time when the solitary hand, once more, comes to rest upon that grinning skull and I shall have to make my way down to the grim black river and await the coming of the dark boatman.

But what will be my dire fate when He comes and I have no coin with which to pay Him? To what infernal hell will I be consigned — or will it be my lot to be refused that final journey across the Styx, forcing me to live out an eternity in this grim old house on the edge of the cliffs?

2

Aunt Amelia

I had terrifying dreams about the episode for a long time after it all happened — the kind of nightmare where you find yourself in a dark room in a place where you know for certain there is no one else and then the door begins to open slowly and something, not fully visible, enters. You make desperate efforts to scream, to do something to release the awful tension inside you but nothing comes out — nothing can stop that thing from coming in — and I always woke with a bubbling, inarticulate groan on my lips, shivering and sweating.

It all began when I received a letter from my Aunt Amelia. It came at a time when I was working long hours for a pitifully low wage and when she suggested I should go and stay with her as she was now old and lonely with no other living relative, I thought seriously about her proposition.

I had not seen Aunt Amelia for almost twenty years. My last and only visit to her rambling old house deep in the country had been at the age nine and we had corresponded only once or twice in the interim. My vague childhood memories of her were of a tall, slender woman, white-haired, always elegantly dressed, with prim, though attractive, features. A woman who lived alone in the big house except for a manservant even older than herself.

Receiving her invitation quite out of the blue surprised me. Undoubtedly, she would be set in her ways although her handwriting was a good indication that she was still in possession of all her faculties. The letters were also far bolder than I would have expected of anyone her age.

However, common sense told me I had nothing to lose by accepting and as far as the material things of this world were concerned, providing companionship to a woman who could only have a few years left might leave me, as her only heir, quite comfortably well off in a very short time.

Accordingly, I gave in my notice and the next day took the train for Exeter and then a rattling old taxi to the house, half a mile from Twyford, arriving there just as dusk was falling. Walking up the path to her door, I suddenly found myself back in the past, back almost a quarter of a century, to when I had first seen the house. All of those memories came flooding back as I saw, to my surprise, that nothing seemed to have changed. The flower-filled borders and the small wooden gate at the side of the house, leading into the apple orchard where the trees were in full blossom.

The low stone walls which formed the perimeter of the grounds and the old-fashioned wicker gate which led around the lee of the hill to the ancient cemetery. They were all there. I recalled how frightened I had been when she had insisted on taking me there, moving among the headstones and inside the dark, somber church with the stern figures outlined in coloured glass and leaden strips in the high windows.

My sense of shock and unpreparedness was compounded when Aunt Amelia met me at the door. For an instant, I really believed that, by some trick of time, I was in reality back in those distant days. I had expected to find a frail old lady, bent and twisted, with wrinkled features, possibly confined to a wheelchair. Instead, the woman who stood waving to greet me was still tall and straight.

'Welcome, James,' she said. 'It was good of you to accept my invitation. I trust you had a pleasant journey.' She stood on one side to allow me to enter, following and closing the door behind her.

'Very pleasant,' I managed to say.

'Good. I'll show you to your room. Everything is ready for you. Then you must come down and have something to eat. I'm sure we have a lot to talk about. Why, it's such a long time since you were here with your parents and you've changed so much I hardly know you.'

'If you'll forgive me for saying so, Aunt Amelia,' I replied, 'but you don't seem to have altered at all.'

She led the way up the wide stairway, saying over her shoulder, 'I suppose it's living here that keeps the years at bay. It's so very peaceful. None of the worries you younger people have nowadays.'

Opening the door at the end of the corridor, she showed me inside, pausing just inside the doorway. 'When you've settled in, come down and let me hear all your news.'

Supper was laid out on the large oak table in the dining room when I went downstairs a quarter of an hour later. While I ate ravenously, she plied me with questions regarding my work and how I had fared over the years since she had last seen me. When I had finished, I leaned back and lit a cigarette while she talked about herself.

She began with all the friends she had known in the past, all of whom were now either dead and buried in the nearby graveyard, or had moved away from the district and no longer bothered to communicate with her.

When I asked about Jenkins, the

manservant, there was a short hiatus in the conversation. Then she said abruptly: 'I'd rather not talk about him, James, if you don't mind. I employed him for more than thirty years and then he simply left. No notice or warning. He just went out one night and never came back.'

'Didn't you make any inquiries? Perhaps he took ill. After all, he was very old.'

Aunt Amelia sniffed. 'Why should I have done? If he wanted to desert me after all those years, then good riddance.'

'And no one comes in to help you?'

'I don't need help and I expect you to make yourself useful. You won't mind that, will you?' She glanced at the large ornamental clock above the fireplace. It was almost eleven-thirty. We had been talking for nearly two hours. 'It's getting late. You must be tired after that long journey.'

In spite of my weariness, I did not fall asleep immediately. It was a warm, sultry night with no wind to bring any coolness even though the window was open. For some reason, I felt decidedly uneasy even though I could find no reason for it.

I was just dropping off to sleep when a sudden sound brought me fully awake. It was the sound of the front door being opened and closed quietly. I knew my aunt was the only other person in the house and wondered where she could be going at that time of night.

Slipping out of bed, I padded to the door, crossed the corridor into one of the other rooms which overlooked the front of the house, and drew back the thick curtains a fraction. A wash of moonlight flooded the grounds and, a few moments later, I made out my aunt. She was walking swiftly and purposefully towards the far side of the garden, not once looking right or left. I watched as she passed through the gate and from my vantage point it was quite easy to see over the low wall and in the bright moonlight everything was as clear as day.

There was no doubt in my mind where she was going — to the old graveyard just beyond the hill where I could see the square tower of the church silhouetted against the sky. I remained there for the best part of half an hour, keeping a close watch, but there was no sign of her returning.

All sorts of weird ideas raced through my mind during my vigil. Whatever the purpose of her nocturnal trip, I could find no reason for it. Certainly some of her old friends would be buried there but why visit their graves during the night?

In the morning when I came down to breakfast, I found her seated at the table. Everything had been prepared and, surprisingly, she did not look in the least tired despite clearly having been up all night.

'Did you sleep well, James?' she asked sweetly. 'Sometimes it can be difficult getting to sleep in a new place.'

'I slept like a log,' I lied. 'I woke up only once. Some sound must have disturbed me but I've no idea what it was.'

She smiled at me across the table. 'There are all kinds of noises in the country which you aren't used to living in the town.'

After breakfast, she said, 'There's

something I want you to do for me.'

'Just name it,' I replied.

'I intend to take up a little hobby, something that has fascinated me for some time. I want to make some rubbings of the old engravings in the church. It's very old, you know. Goes back to Norman times with such a lot of history attached to it.'

'I'm glad you've found something to occupy your mind,' I told her, although I could scarcely imagine her going down on her hands and knees on the stone floor of the church. 'What is it you want me to do?'

'I need some carbon sticks and paper. You can get both in the village. There's a little shop there near the square and I'm sure they'll have them.'

'I'll go right away. I need some more cigarettes anyway.'

The day was sunny and warm but with a cooling breeze which made walking pleasant. I located the shop without difficulty and taking my purchases to the counter, the middle-aged owner totted them up.

'You're a stranger in these parts,' he said conversationally. 'Are you living in the Village?'

'No. I'm staying with my aunt, Amelia Dexter.'

'Miss Dexter.' There was a note of astonishment in his voice. 'I never knew she had any relations.'

Since the man seemed disposed to talk, there being no one else in the shop, I asked, 'Did you know her manservant?'

'Jenkins? Certainly I knew him. He often came into the village for things. Your aunt used to come in once or twice but I haven't seen her for some time.'

'Do you know what happened to him?'

The man scratched his chin pensively. He seemed a little reluctant to reply. Then, leaning forward with his elbows on the counter, he said, 'It was a real funny business. Happened a few years ago. A couple of farmers spotted him not far from the cemetery. Must've been some time after midnight, from what I've heard. He was wandering around in the pouring rain, completely out of his mind. God alone knows what happened to him.

'They took him to Doctor Willoughby who had him committed to some asylum. Either he's dead now, or still there. Far as I know, they never got a sensible word out of him.'

For a moment, something cold and clammy brushed along my spine. Then it was gone. 'Something must have frightened him,' I said.

'No doubt about that,' the owner affirmed. 'But whatever it was, no one will ever know.' He glanced down at the articles I had bought. 'You interested in drawing?'

I shook my head. 'These are for my aunt. She's taking up collecting rubbings from the church.'

'Well, I suppose there's no accounting for taste,' he said thoughtfully. 'But it seems an odd pastime for a lady of her age. Wish her luck from me.'

Aunt Amelia was sitting, sunning herself, in the garden when I got back. She took the paper and carbon sticks, then said, 'I think I'll go to the church this afternoon. The weather seems to be holding and there'll be no one there. I won't disturb anyone and no one will disturb me. The vicar can be a little fussy about these things, you know.'

'I'm sure he wouldn't mind you engaging in your hobby.' I replied.

'Still, I'd rather he knew nothing about it for the moment.' She glanced up as she spoke and I had the impression that her statement was a veiled warning to me not to mention it to anyone.

While she sat on the lawn I went into the garden shed, took out a pair of shears, and proceeded to prune the back hedge at the rear of the house. The job took me the best part of two hours, sweeping up the cuttings and depositing them in one comer.

When I returned, her chair was still there, but empty. I decided she had already gone to the church and went inside to make myself something to eat. I knew when she set her mind on something, she would go through with it to the bitter end and brook no interference.

It was growing dark when she came back. Sitting in the front room, I heard the door open and she came in, carrying the rolls of paper under one arm. For some reason, she seemed irritable.

Placing the rubbings on the table, she lit two more candles for there was no electricity in the house, then unrolled a couple, placing two paperweights at each end to hold them flat.

'Tell me,' she said harshly. 'What do you make of them?'

I studied the rubbings in the candlelight. I knew little of these things but, sensing her mood, I said, 'They seem excellent. Are all of these from the church?'

'Most are around the walls which makes it very difficult. I have to hold the paper with one hand and it's not easy to prevent it slipping but I think I've got them right. It's these others, the important ones, where I had the greatest difficulty.'

While speaking, she had pulled two further sheets of paper from those she had made.

'There are old tombs in the church, you know, beneath the aisle. Those are the ones I wanted to be perfect. But they kept moving!'

I stared at her I knew she was extremely meticulous in everything she did, that everything had to be just right, but I could not understand what she was getting at.

'They kept moving?' I asked finally.

'The brass plates, of course,' she snapped.

'But surely brass plates on the floor don't move,' I said. 'What would cause them to do that?'

'Don't patronize me, James.' Her voice suddenly took on a brittle edge. 'I have absolutely no idea of the cause but those plates kept moving whenever I tried to make my rubbing.'

Trying to calm her, I said, 'Perhaps if I was to come with you, we could try to find out what's happening. Some of these very old buildings suffer from subsidence and — '

'Subsidence, of course. Why didn't I think of that? The church is in a dreadful state, hasn't been repaired for years. I'm surprised it hasn't collapsed into a ruin years ago.'

I looked again at the rubbings.

Certainly the two she had indicated were less distinct than the others. It was barely possible to make out the details.

In my own mind, I knew that whatever had been the cause, subsidence was out of the question. That church had stood for almost two millennia and its foundations were as solid as rock. It was clear, however, that as far as she was concerned, the subject was closed. Gathering up the rubbings, she rolled them up carefully and placed them in a large cupboard.

Remembering the events of the previous night, I deliberately remained awake after going to bed. My aunt's bedroom was just along the corridor and I was sure I would hear her if she went out again. By the time one o' clock came and there had been no sound, I decided she was probably asleep but then, just as I was preparing to relax, a faint sound reached me.

There was the soft click of a door opening. Instantly, I opened my door, just in time to glimpse her white-clad figure moving down the stairs. Pausing at the top of the stairs, I waited until I heard the front door close, then ran to the porch and out into the open. She was there, some fifty yards away, slipping through the gate. Wherever she was going, whatever she meant to do, this time I was going to be there.

By the time I reached the gate leading into the churchyard, she was nowhere to be seen. Then a sudden movement caught my attention. She was standing in the shadow of a massive yew on the far side of the churchyard.

It was difficult to see her clearly since she was almost hidden by the intervening headstones but she appeared to be talking to herself — or was she speaking to whoever lay within the earth?

I went no further. I knew I would be intruding upon something either very personal — or upon something far more terrible, and at that moment I had no wish to find out which of those surmises was correct.

Going back to my room, I undressed and tried to get some sleep. Aunt Amelia had still not returned.

I felt oddly drained and lethargic the

next day. What little sleep I'd had during the night had been sporadic and unrefreshing. Nevertheless I knew I had to do something otherwise I would find myself dwelling upon things I didn't want to think about.

I decided to paint the gutters around the front of the house while my aunt went over the rubbings she had made the previous day. Finding a long ladder against the side of the shed, I located a couple of tins of paint and a large brush and made myself busy for the whole of the morning.

It was while I was cleaning my hands with turpentine that I noticed the door in the corner that I dimly recalled led down into the cellar. I looked around for the key, which I remembered having been hung on a high nail beside the door. The nail was still there, rusty now, but there was no sign of the key. Trying the door, I found it to be securely locked. The key might have been lost, and I was relying on memories of twenty years earlier, but something about its absence disturbed me.

Going into the front room, I asked Aunt Amelia about it but she merely replied that it must have gone missing a long time before. Certainly she could not recall seeing it for several years.

'There's nothing down there anyway,' she added. 'Why do you ask?'

'Nothing really,' I replied. 'I just thought I'd tidy it up for you and get rid of anything you no longer need.'

'No need to bother your head about that. You'll be better occupied getting the exterior of the house done before winter comes.'

That evening, it began to rain, a steady downpour that continued for the next three days. My aunt fretted continually at not being able to go along to the church and continue with her hobby, flitting restlessly about the house, peering out of the windows to check on the weather.

Then, on the fourth day, two things happened which were to bring the horror to a head. The weather cleared suddenly. The sun blazed from a cloudless blue sky and Aunt Amelia announced her intention of making further rubbings of the brass plates set in the stone pavings inside the church.

It was also the morning when, hunting among some old tins at the back of the garden shed, I discovered the large, rusty key for which I had been searching. Slipping it into my pocket, I went into the house.

Aunt Amelia was already dressed for going out and, recalling our earlier discussion, I said I would accompany her, just to see for myself what happened when she made her rubbings of the plates over the tombs.

I half expected her to make some protest but she merely said, 'Come if you like, James. Then you can see for yourself.'

Together, we walked through the churchyard to the church. It was cool and dim inside, the rows of pews standing empty on either side.

'Now where are those plates?' I asked as we paused in the doorway.

'Over here.' She led the way towards the altar, then stopped and pointed at her feet.

There were, indeed, two plaques set in the stone floor. The lettering on both was barely legible. The passage of innumerable feet had worn them almost smooth. Going down on my hands and knees, I ran my fingers over the plates. Despite the way they had been effaced by time, I reckoned the lettering should have shown up more clearly on the rubbings that my aunt had made several days before.

I felt a little strange, kneeling there, knowing that directly beneath me were the bones of Sir Roger and Lady Elwyn de Courtney, buried there in the middle of the sixteenth century. Scrambling to my feet, I sat down on one of the pews.

'Are you all right, James?' Aunt Amelia asked concernedly. 'You do look a little queer.'

'I'm fine,' I replied. 'It's just the chill in here after the heat outside.'

'Then you just sit there while I get on with my work.' She had brought a small cushion with her and placing it carefully on the stone, she sank down onto her knees, spreading the sheet of paper over the brass.

A sudden, muttered exclamation from my aunt brought my attention to her. I saw the look of exasperated consternation on her face as she straightened abruptly from her work. The rubbing was half finished.

'What is it?' I asked, keeping my voice down.

'It's just the same as before,' she complained. 'Just when I think I have it, everything starts moving.'

If my aunt had been any other type of person; I would have thought she was imagining things. As it was, she threw down her carbon stick with an angry motion and gestured me down beside her.

'There — feel it,' she commanded.

To please her, I placed my right hand on top of the paper where it covered the brass plate. I could feel nothing out of the ordinary and opened my mouth to say so. But then, picking up the carbon stick she began moving it lightly across the paper. Almost at once, I felt the plate beneath my hand begin to shake. With a faint cry, I snatched my hand away.

'There, what did I tell you?' she said

triumphantly. 'You felt it too, didn't you?'
'I felt something,' I admitted.
'Like a shaking beneath the paving.'
'Something like that.' I felt a little tremor of fear pass through me. What the hell was going on? I did not believe in spirits or any other ghostly phenomenon. Yet I had distinctly felt that movement beneath my hand.

Straightening up, I said harshly, 'I don't think you should go on with this, Aunt Amelia. Forget this little hobby for the time being.'

She shook her head vehemently. 'No, I'll be damned if I'm going to let anything stop me. If they don't like what I'm doing, that's just too bad.'

I did not try to stop her. I just stood there, shivering for a few moments, knowing there was something unnatural going on but not knowing what it was. All I knew was that I had no wish to remain in that old church. She was still on her hands and knees, rubbing away viciously, as I turned and left.

I knew she would remain there for some hours once she went into one of her moods of perverse obstinacy. Accordingly, I decided to check on the cellar in her absence.

Lighting a candle, I unlocked the cellar door and pulled it open. It was clear no one had been down there for a long time and I descended the steps slowly; holding the candle in front of me.

Finally, I reached the bottom, shielding the candle flame with one hand as I bent to peer into the darkness. As I looked for a place to put the candle, I noticed something dark and misshapen lying on the dusty floor. Lowering the candle, the light fell full upon the object and the scream that came unbidden to my lips echoed eerily around the confining walls.

There was no mistaking the features even though the skin was parchment dry and brittle.

It was Aunt Amelia!

There was no doubt the body had been there for a considerable time. In that horrifying moment it was as if all I had subconsciously conjectured, what I had forced deep into the back of my thoughts, what I had not wanted to face, had all come together in that single instant of clarity.

I could not doubt the evidence of my own eyes. How she had died, there was no way of knowing. Whether it had been a tragic accident, or deliberate murder on the part of Jenkins, a sudden push as she had stood at the top. All I did know was that, ever since arriving at the house, I had been in the presence of a ghost, that my aunt would haunt this place for ever, and the longer I remained there with this horror, the more difficult it would be to escape.

All of the signs had been there had I opened my eyes to see them. Her vigils in the churchyard, speaking with the spirits of those friends who had gone before. That queer shaking above the tombs of the dead in her presence.

Before she returned I had thrown all of my things into the two cases and left by the back way, circling around through the woods. Two hours later, I caught the train to London.

Now all I have left are the dreams, which still haunt my sleep — nightmares from which I wake screaming and shaking uncontrollably.

But more than that, there is the thought that, someday, a letter will come, informing me that my aunt's body has been discovered and that, as her only heir, I must go to claim my inheritance — to find her waiting at the door to greet me with that terrible knowing smile on her lips as she did once before!

3

That Deep Black Yonder

On September 26, 1932, I took the express train from Paddington and began the four-hour long journey that was to take me to the Devon coast and into a nightmare of horror from which the doctors say I shall never fully recover. That I did not witness any actual visual horror until the very end made the mental shock only more terrifying, the final episode in a series of such events which sent me running through the wind-scoured, storm-ridden night along the cliff tops with the stinging rain lashing my face and the pounding waves of the Atlantic lit by vivid flashes of lightning that tore the berserk heavens apart.

For three months, I had lain seriously ill in a hospital in north London, recovering from a major operation and this had been followed by a similar length of time convalescing at my home in Chelsea. That summer in London had been exceptionally hot and oppressive and my physician, Doctor Forsyth, had seen that my recovery was hampered rather than accelerated by the heat. When the beginning of September had brought no alleviation, he suggested that a change of air and scenery would prove beneficial. Sea air, he maintained, was all I needed to regain my health and strength and a holiday in Cornwall had been his suggestion, one I had readily fallen in with since I had grown to hate and detest the dusty streets of London during the long, drought-filled summer with the parks full of trees burned and ugly brown, the usual green grass patchy for want of moisture.

My letter of enquiry to an estate agent in Bude had been answered almost by return with information that an old manor house was available at a modest rent on the shore between Bude and Morwenstow. It occupied a somewhat isolated position on the cliffs, but I did not let this fact deter me. From the news given in the letter it seemed the ideal place for me. I had always been of a solitary disposition, preferring to keep my own company, shunning crowds; and even at the end of September there was the possibility of holiday-makers flooding into the Devon and Cornish coastal towns.

It was early afternoon when I was admitted to the offices of Swatheley & Corrie, Estate Agents. Arnold Swatheley proved to be a short, balding affable man in his early fifties who readily agreed to drive me out to Faxted Manor once I had affirmed my desire to rent it for an indefinite period.

As we made our way along the narrow, winding road which skirted the top of the cliffs most of the way, only occasionally moving inland so far that it was out of sight of the sea, he explained that the manor had been occupied only intermittently during the past century. It was now almost forty years since the last owner had packed up and left for South Africa. There had been talk of a personal tragedy which had struck the Harcroft family, something unspeakable that had been all but forgotten now down the intervening years. All attempts to reach the survivors of the family had met with no success, as had attempts to find a buyer for the property once the courts had presumed them dead.

So Faxted Manor remained untenanted throughout the whole of the forty years. A platoon of soldiers had been billeted there for three weeks during the World War, sometime in the winter of 1917, but after three men had unaccountably disappeared, gone over the cliffs one wild night according to the information Swatheley had, the platoon had left and the manor brooded alone among the white cliffs, with only the wild seabirds to keep it company and the rollers beating their heads on the rocks below. Not that its existence had gone unnoticed during all of those years. Students of the mediaeval history of this part of the country had come to examine its structure. The architecture was quaint, a combination of several styles, Gothic towers had been built on to a far earlier base, though now little remained of this older structure. Extensive renovations had been carried out in the time of the Harcroft tenancy, obliterating much of the earlier work.

My first sight of Faxted Manor evoked little emotion in me. We rounded a sharp bend in the narrow road and there it lay before us, sunken a little beneath the towering, grey-white cliffs that rose on all sides of it as if somehow trying to hide it from view. It stood within fifty yards of the cliff edge where the rocky walls plunged almost vertically for two hundred feet into the frothing water that spumed and foamed on to the needle-shaped rocks, and I saw that the road led directly to the front of the house and no further.

As we drew closer to the manor, however, I felt a sudden stir of anticipation, after the way of a man who had somehow discovered something he had never dreamed of, and there was a faint ruffling of the small hairs on the back of my neck as if a chill wind had blown from the direction of the house. As we got out of the car, I had the unshakeable feeling that Swatheley was affected in the same manner, possibly even more so than myself. He appeared oddly hesitant to enter the place, opening the door with a key that grated in the lock, standing back so that I might go in first.

The current of air that came from inside the building at the opening of that door was a sudden noxious rush of decay as at the opening of a tomb. We did not pause long in the doorway but went inside, into a long hall, panelled and hung with pictures half-hidden in dust and filmy cobwebs. Very little daylight filtered in through the grimed windows. The dust on the floor of the hall was a thick grey carpet. The rest of the house was composed of vast and dismal chambers; some of them with torn, mildewed hangings which all but covered the walls, dark passages and high ceilings, arched and carved, most of the carvings hideous in the extreme, possessing a curiously *unearthly* quality that sent a little shiver along my nerves. There was an air of dampness about the place, too, but I knew that a few roaring fires in the wide hearths would soon rid the room of this and I felt suddenly calm and content there.

I could see that Swatheley was surprised by my attitude, that he had expected me to turn and flee the instant I saw the manor. Whether he considered I was mad or not it was difficult to say, but his gaze was curious when I finally told him that I would take the place for the coming winter and asked whether it would be possible to obtain servants to live in since, with the autumn and winter coming, the storms which ranged along the strip of coast of a terrible violence would prevent anyone from getting there and back each day.

Swatheley agreed to do his best for me but made it clear that he would have to go further afield than Bude, or anywhere in the near vicinity since the people around of those parts would have nothing whatever to do with the place, having an almost unbelievable aversion and hatred of the manor and all associated with it. As if to emphasise the difficulty of getting anyone, and pointing out that it would be almost impossible for me to remain there long, he suggested I should put up at the hotel in Bude until he had made the necessary arrangements which he assured me would be only a matter of a few days.

What made me fall in so readily with this plan was my desire to learn more of the history of the manor and since I understood that one of the scholars who had been studying the place for almost three years was living in Bude, it would afford me an excellent opportunity for discussing it with him.

During the week I stayed in Bude, I met George Carrington on several occasions. He was a reticent, raw-boned individual, a product of Oxford, who seemed a trifle out of place outside the cloisters of the University. He was only too willing to express his own opinions and tell me some of the tales which circulated in the district concerning Faxted Manor, initially, perhaps hoping to dissuade me from staying there, an act which he considered to be the height of folly. When he saw that I was determined to go through with my plans, he ceased his attempts to make me change my mind. I gained the impression he was only too pleased to find someone willing to listen to him; that his original intention had been to publish his findings in one of the journals devoted to such outworldly tales, but that he had eventually been forced to the conclusion that these stories were so ghastly and terrifying he had decided against such a course.

Typical as the tales were, speaking of evil rites that had been performed in the manor since early in the Fourteenth Century, possibly far earlier than that — although the more remote history was shrouded in the mists of antiquity and only scattered fragments remained in existence — they did not repel me as Carrington clearly expected. Rather I found them to be oddly stimulating, exciting my imagination. One theme ran persistently through the accounts that had been handed down verbally through the ages. Something unutterably evil had either existed in the house in remote times, or had been born into the Warhope family — or *Warr Hoppe* — as it had been known during the Fourteenth

Century. There were accounts of strange pestilences, which had affected the surrounding countryside, of terrible and abnormal growths that had sprouted up from the once fertile soil on top of the cliffs and a little to landward; and of things that had been cast ashore on wintry nights on to the narrow strip of sandy beach at the foot of the cliffs whenever the storms raged along the coast. Carrington had carried out extensive investigations into the possible identity of these odd remains but with only a limited success. A search among the church records going back for almost four hundred years had revealed isolated, but cunningly concealed, accounts of creatures buried in unhallowed ground or taken out in boats at dead of night and thrown into the sea, but these records were, he felt sure, merely hints of other things, dark and evil things, spawned out of pits deep and remote and unimaginable.

In one ancient chronicle, there was reference to the marriage of one Henry Warhope to Nylene Poiseder in 1521, a union that appeared to have lasted less than a year, ending with Henry Warhope being tried for the abominable murder of his wife. What had been brought to light during the trial by his peers was not given in the chronicle, but the verdict had been a complete acquittal for the condemned man.

'There was something given in the evidence then which they did not repeat to the outside world,' Carrington said. 'Something the church prohibited. This fact, that so many things have been deliberately hidden and suppressed, is the most annoying thing about the whole business. It can be explained on the assumption that there is nothing more to this than the ramblings of superstitious peasants or, as I believe, the events were of such a nauseous nature, were so far *outside* even the knowledge of the church and the learned men of that period, that they had no other course open to them.'

I assured him I was not in the least perturbed by the stories, even if, in those far-off days, they may have held an element of truth. These things belonged to the realm of spectral lore and at that time, I was a pronounced sceptic in such matters. Those who search after vague and unspecified horrors spoke of how old legends will often haunt strange, out-of-the-way places; go down into black, slime-covered vaults where catacombs are hewn out of the solid rock wall; linger by moon-infested night in haunted rooms and turrets where sky-rearing towers thrust spectral fingers to a cloud-wracked sky. They see dark, lycanthropic like figures that flicked through forests of hideous trees among the Hartz Mountains, or midnight things silhouetted against the face of the moon and hidden by day in rotting coffins tucked away from prying eyes in vaults deep beneath the vampire-ridden Rhine castles.

During the six days I spent in Bude, I learned all that Carrington had discovered concerning Faxted Manor and by the end of my stay, had pieced together a reasonably full story of the house's black medieval history from the date when the first records were available, to the time when the last occupiers had left, suddenly, and for some unknown reason.

Then, on October 3, 1932, I moved into the manor. Three servants had been found who were agreeable to remain there with me, all of them from Truro, far enough afield for them not to have been affected by any of the wild rumours that were still rife concerning the place. William Pengarden had been a seaman for most of his fifty-three years, was a solid and very intense man, strong and obedient and dependable. Mary Ventnor, who combined the duties of cook and maid, was a tall girl of twenty-six, not given to listening to these tales of wild fancy as also was Carfax, a man in his late thirties, sullen by nature, but robust and unimaginative. None of the three appeared concerned by the isolated nature of the manor and if any of them had heard the curious stories, which circulated in the district, they either ignored them, or kept them to themselves.

For almost two weeks, the general routine at Faxted Manor proceeded evenly and with a quiet placidity, my own time being spent mainly in poring through the old, moth-eaten documents which filled the shelves of the library in the West Wing. It may well be imagined how powerfully I was affected by these records when I discovered that many of them had been preserved from the earliest days of the house, were possibly priceless volumes, giving a graphic account of the happenings of those distant days. The picture provided by these writings, adding much to that which I had learnt from Carrington, was not one designed to set my mind at rest concerning the evil reputation the place possessed.

Before, the vague tales had been extremely picturesque and fanciful, most of them based on hearsay carried down and embellished through the long centuries. But the records here were of a different kind altogether, giving a consistent and onerously continual record of the house from the Eighth Century when a stone building had been erected on the site by an order of monks who had flourished there until their diabolical rites had forced the king, Edgar, to put an end to their heathen practices in 966. The monastery had been razed to the ground and after a short trial, the members of the order, without exception, had been hurled off the top of the cliff into the sea. There were dark hints in the documents of the relics which had been found buried in narrow passages beneath the site, of human and inhuman remains discovered in the lower chambers hewn out of the solid rock and there was a general feeling of relief in the neighbourhood, and a belief that a terrible evil which had overshadowed them, had been destroyed forever.

The area was apparently shunned, or at least disregarded, until the lands were given to William de Warr Hoppe in 1124 by Henry I, who built the forerunner of the present manor on the clifftop. For close on a hundred and fifty years there was no record of any trace of evil associated with the place, nor anything sinister about the family, who occupied. Then, in 1271, John Warr Hoppe extended the building by erecting the West Wing, covering the site of the ancient monastery and the first inkling of the impending calamity that was to follow the family for more than six hundred years, showed itself. Having married in the previous year, their first child, a girl, died five months after birth of a sickly malady, which defied all analysis. Of the four other children of this union, two were stillborn, both girls, while the sons apparently thrived.

But the family seemed cursed after that. There were attestations of strange ailments which afflicted the Warr Hoppes, of mutant children born into the family, shut away in the curious stone cells which had been hollowed out under the foundations some hundreds of years earlier, of frightening *inhuman* cries heard in the night, of nocturnal excursions made to the shore during the moonless eldritch hours; blue-green lights which flickered behind untapestried windows, horrific black shapes outlined therein, and a return of the old and half-forgotten pestilences to the district, with evil shrouding the area and abounding a hundredfold.

In 1797, Cecil Warhope, in his fiftieth year, went inexplicably mad and wandered into the village of Morganswode, as it was known then, giving voice to strange dreams and visions of the most terrible sort which sent a band of men back to the manor bearing flaming torches and carrying any weapons they could lay their hands on. They had found little amiss in the house itself, but down on the narrow stretch of beach at the foot of the cliffs, were odd tracks in the sand which had not been washed away by the encroaching sea, although for the sanity of one or two members of the band of men, it would have been better by far if the tide had obliterated them entirely before they had been found.

In the flickering yellow candlelight, seated in the high-backed chair, before the blazing fire, I read through the tattered and fading parchments backed by peeling leather that was cracked and worn, reading of the finding of William

Warhope, Cecil's brother, on the beach, his body and features curiously deformed, oddly grotesque, mindless horror mirrored in the wide-open eyes that stared up at the moon-flooded heavens. Rather than allow such an obviously unhallowed soul to rest in peace in the quiet ground of the small churchyard, his body had been hastily buried in the sand of the beach and on that same morning, the worst storm in the history of that stretch of coastline broke over the cliffs, seemingly centred on Faxted Manor. Certainly it was unlike anything known in living memory. Most vivid of all, apparently, in the eyes of the unknown chronicler, was a belief, rife at the time among the superstitious peasants on the beach, that after the storm had died down late the following afternoon, another set of prints as bizarre and unbelievable as the first, had appeared in the sand, running almost parallel with the others which had, by that time, been almost washed away; but in this case the prints led up out of the sea and up the sheer wall of the cliff towards Faxted Manor.

The horror had returned with a vengeance.

* * *

Such was the history which assailed me and which I absorbed during the first few days at the manor. It must not, however, be imagined that I spent all my waking hours in the library, reading among these ancient, musty tomes of a bygone age. The weather at that time proved to be exceedingly clement even for early October and I spent much time out of doors, taking as much of the fresh air as possible. Several times, I wandered to the edge of the rocks and stared down their almost vertical depths to where the sea crashed onto the boulders in a spuming of white, wind-tossed spray. There was, I noticed, a small promontory where a ridge of cliff thrust itself out into the sea for perhaps fifty yards, forming a natural breakwater there, enclosing a tiny bay where the water seemed calmer than further out, or even a little way along the coast.

Towards late evening during the second week of my stay there, I often stood on top of the cliffs looking out to the west where some of the most unusual and colourful sunsets I had ever known occurred with an almost clockwork regularity. One particular evening proved no exception. The entire sky to the west was a mass of pinks and scarlet, blending imperceptibly into apple green, blue and finally purple directly overhead. Lowering my glance from the flaming wonders of the sunset, I chanced to look down at the water immediately below me and felt an odd edge of surprise to notice that on this occasion, the surface within the tiny bay was not smooth and unruffled as it normally was. There was something thrusting itself up above the water. From where I stood, in the fading light, it looked rather like a black stone monolith, its lower half hidden by the waves. I wished I had brought my binoculars with me so that I might have examined it more closely for there seemed to be strange carvings on it, but with the night falling, I had to reluctantly give up any attempt to discover the exact nature of the object.

That night I retired early. I had not yet fully recovered from my long illness and the long walk along the cliffs coupled with the hours spent during the past week poring over the old manuscripts into the early hours of the morning had tired me more than I had realised.

My room was in the west wing of the house, high in one turreted tower, the solitary window looking out directly over the small bay alongside the narrow headland. It was reached by a winding stairway of stone, between walls that still ran with dripping moisture in spite of the fires that had been lit.

I fell asleep as soon as my head touched the pillow but was soon haunted by dreams of the most hideous kind. I was standing alone on the wind-swept cliffs looking down into the twilight sea. The water heaved with a sullen, oily swell, black and fathomless; yet there was something in those dark depths and vast deeps, something which was straining to the surface, unutterably evil, a thing which was not of Earth, had no part in anything that was sane and normal. There was the vaguest suspicion of moonlight in the sky and as I turned in my dream to where the house should have stood, I discovered myself staring at a circle of crudely-hewn stones of the most terrifying aspect, lit by the grotesque paleness of the moonlight. There were presences in among the stones; queer, half-visible things that hovered and flitted on the edge of my vision, never coming close enough, nor staying still long enough, to be seen clearly and all the more frightening because of this abnormal, spectral elusiveness.

One thing in particular I noticed in my dream. A creature that stood hooded and gowned, on the cliff edge, arms raised as if in supplication. Then it turned and it was as if I screamed aloud in my dream. It would be wrong to say that this monstrosity, visible as the hood which covered its face fell back at that instant, could not be described in terms understandable by anyone who had knowledge of these black abominations from pits unimaginable and unnameable. There was something human about it but if anything it was this merest hint of *humanness* that brought the sense of terror crowding into my sleeping mind. The protruding forehead was ridged and furrowed and the two bony protuberances gave an unmistakable sense of witnessing some fiendish creature from the lowest pit of Hell. Some instinct warned me, even in the dream, that what I was witnessing here had no connection with the present day.

The being began to mumble and mutter and there was nothing English in the mouthings, indeed the disjointed phrases seemed to have no earthly connotation and as they trailed off into nothingness, something stirred deep within the black water below the cliff. There was a swirling as if a whirlpool was forming; a surging, leprous gleaming of spectral whiteness, indistinct at first, then growing clearer as it came up to the surface. I felt my gaze drawn hypnotically to the sea where the waves, whipped to a sudden frenzy, hammered on the belt of sand that fronted the rocks. Then it emerged, dripping, from the sea and whatever horror, whatever frenzy of nightmarish terror I had experienced before, faded into insignificance before the soul-searing fear which took a hold of my sleeping mind.

Shivering intolerably, with the clammy sweat lying cold on my body, I woke with a start, my heart palpitating wildly in my chest. Hands clutching at my body, I opened my eyes, peered about me.

The most terrible, the most unbelievable of all mental shocks is that of the totally unexpected. The nightmare was still strong in my mind, the shaking still lay on my limbs from the sheer terror of it but nothing in that dream could compare with the fear I now felt as I saw what lay about me; not the simple furnishings of my room high in the turreted tower, nor even the long, winding stairway which led up to it — but the rocky, moss-turfed cliffs with the dark silhouette of the manor more than a hundred yards away and the dull booming in my ears, blending with the tortuous beating of my heart, was the sound of the sea breaking on the rocks.

I cannot even begin to hint at the thoughts that went through my mind as I stumbled back to the manor. The main door opened creakingly at my touch and this was evidently the means by which I had earlier left the house. How long had passed since I had left my room and gone wandering forth into the night, I could not tell but I knew that if I did not get warm at once. I would, in my weakened state, run a distinct risk of catching pneumonia. Throwing a handful of logs on to the fire, which had burned down to mere glowing embers, I sat in front of it until the wood caught and blazed up slowly, very slowly, as the heat permeated into my chilled body. Gradually, the fear in my shocked, numbed mind, subsided.

It had been nothing more than a dream, of course, a highly vivid dream possibly the result of the excitement which had been building up inside me over the past few days and the general malaise had brought about our recurrence of the sleep-walking which had once afflicted me as a child.

Further sleep that night was utterly out

of the question, so lighting the long candle I sat in the high-backed chair by the fire, threw a heavy wrap over my legs and waited for the dawn. As I sat there, I became aware of the noises in the house. It was the first time I had really noticed them. Before, they had been mere background sounds. Now there was an oddly menacing tone to them; a moaning, droning whisper, which built up from some inconceivable depth beneath the structure of the manor, an ululation that sent shivers along my taut-strung nerves. The sound persisted until the first greys and blues of the dawn showed through the windows, then it subsided to a soft, hideous murmur that never quite faded into nothingness.

That morning, I summoned the two men and asked them to bring lanterns, so that I might examine the vaults and cellars of the house. At the bottom of a score of stone steps, which led down into an abysmal darkness was a small cellar, the floor slime-covered to a depth of almost two inches, walls glistening in the lantern light, the cracks in the stone filled with horrible fungoid growths, pale and sickly, which had never seen the light of day. The stench that rose around us was full of rottenness and decay and here and there, ranged on narrow shelves around the walls were oddly shaped wooden boxes whose contents I dared not imagine. Was this a part of the old house, built innumerable ages before the manor itself? What I saw there forced me to the inescapable conclusion that it was — and yet, towards the far end of the cellar we came upon a heavy stone slab set in the wall, around the edges of which a faint stirring of air flickered the lantern flames and gave a hint of something more which lay beyond.

Setting our fingers around the edges of the stone we pulled with all of our strength, but for long moments the heavy stone refused to budge. Then, with a leaden swinging motion it moved around a central pivot. The rush of fetid air brought a rising nausea into my stomach. But it was a sensation I instantly forced down in the faint excitement of what lay before me, dimly lit by the pale yellow glow of the lantern I thrust forward.

As I stood there hesitating, I felt I was on the brink of frightful and terrible revelations. The sense of malignancy in that blast of air from those unknown regions had touched me more deeply than I had imagined. The servants, seeing my hesitation, were all for going back, declaring that whatever lay down there, deep in the bowels of the solid rock beneath the manor, it was not good to know. There were many things, they maintained, it was better to remain in utter ignorance of, rather than bring them to light. But as always, my belief that there had to be a logical and scientific explanation for any of the seemingly abnormal and paranormal phenomena, insisted that we should go on and ordering them to follow, I stepped forward, the man at the rear carrying the other lantern.

Slowly, I began the descent into that passage composed of small steps carved from hard rock, steps of such a weirdly impossible shape and design that the mind baulked at any idea of what sort of feet they had been made for in the past. The pale yellow glow revealed, too, that the stone walls were not perfectly smooth but were covered with time-effaced designs, a few of them discernible. Here were the remaining traces of the pictorial art of this long-forgotten age. I paused to look at only a few of them before hurrying on, gagging at the rush of fear in my mind, the muscles of my throat constricted, warning my men not to look at them, knowing that once they did no power on Earth would keep them with me.

Diabolical, like images drawn from some drug-delirium, they were so oddly reminiscent of my dream of the previous night that I could not put them out of my mind. Deeper and deeper went that passage as if we were slipping down some hellish well, through haunted tunnels that rang with the muffling echoes of our feet and oozed a thick, viscid moisture from their walls. I saw, too, that after a while there were other passages leading off from the main one along which we were working our way forward and the lantern light failed to penetrate these black corridors for more than a few feet. Once, I fancied I heard a slithering, rustling sound far off down one of these narrow passages, but as I stopped, my heart thumping madly in my chest, the sound was gone and there was nothing but the gale of our breathing in the stillness.

The tunnel led us down deep within the foundations of the manor and we were soon undoubtedly far inside the rock of the cliff itself. The air here was not wholesome but possessed a horribly fishy odour and it came to me that we must soon be approaching the level of the sea if the tunnel continued to descend in this manner.

The further we proceeded, the more carvings and crude images were in evidence on the walls and there appeared to be some strange pressure effect down there for my ears began to ring painfully. Then, abruptly, without any warning whatsoever, the yellow light from the probing lanterns, which had been reflected from the graven stone walls, vanished and we seemed to be standing in the midst of an inky blackness, unrelieved on all sides, the light failing utterly to pierce the gloom.

The tunnel had opened out into a wide vault; how vast it was, we could not guess. My mind was filled with wild, chaotic thoughts as I stepped haltingly forward, holding the heavy lantern as far above my head as possible but even then it could not illuminate the unknown depths into which we were advancing, for the floor of the great chamber still dipped downward. For several yards, the utter blackness remained impenetrable and then, in a moment of indescribable fear and apprehension, I did see something. At first only a pale glimmering as the faint gleam from the very rim of the circle of lantern-glow touched it, and then seen more clearly, it solidified out of the confining, nightmare gloom. There is no way of conveying any idea of the graven monstrosity stood on top of that hideous altar. Half-reptilian, half-amphibian, it reposed in a semi-crouch and so ready to leap from the stone on to some unsuspecting victim below. Pengarden, immediately behind me, screamed involuntarily as he caught his first glimpse of the thing.

His face was utterly white and flabby, eyes staring from his head. He started back, almost knocking the lantern from Carfax's grasp. Standing there, in the middle of this strange, subterranean world, the image held an air of timeless mystery and horrible suggestion, which was not lost on any of the others. In the light of the lamps, we were able to make out the vague inscriptions carved around the base, making the odd observation that the language used was not ancient English, even of the most archaic kind but some extremely old form of Celtic. Bending forward, we tried to make out something of the letters, to interpret them, but the only fragments that made any kind of sense and sent an indefinable shiver of pure horror through me were vague references to Karyptes. In my early days I had read some of the forbidden writings of the monk, Terrilus, works that had been condemned by the venerable Bede, classed as the impious utterings of a familiar of the Devil.

Karyptes, an obvious Celtic corruption

of the Greek Charybdis, made it impossible for me to entirely suppress a thrill at the knowledge that this great chamber, hewn out of the rock, had been fashioned by hands long dead before the Romans visited the shores of Britain. The well-known line concerning this sea-creature, occurring in the *Alexandreis* of Gautier de Lille, a Twelfth-Century poet: *Incidis in Scyllam cupiend vitare Charybdim*, was known to be at least as old as St. Augustine and according to the condemned treatise of Terrilus, far older.

I made no mention of this to the two men with me, not wishing to alarm them any further, at least until we had explored the great cavern to its furthest extent. Skirting the vast altar we moved on into the enveloping darkness, crossing occasionally from side to side, to feel along the walls and make sure that they still stretched on. Gradually, they began to move inward again as the subterranean chamber narrowed once more and twenty feet further on we came upon a huge door of thick wood, crossed and studded with some kind of metal. But it was not the door itself that brought the ultimate horror to the three of us. There had, for some time, been a vague and curious exhalation of a strongly putrid odour from in front of us and now, as the glow from the lanterns gleamed dully on the door, it had become offensive and more emphatic, sweeping about us in noxious vapours that choked and clogged our throats and lungs. The cause of this unbearable stench could conceivably have been the pile of bones which lay in front of the door, but a moment's glance was sufficient to convince me that these were immeasurably old, some crumbling into dust and it was borne upon me that the source of the stench was something which lay just *beyond* the door.

How long we stood there with the two lanterns lifted high over our heads so that as much of the light as possible fell upon the scene in front of our startled gaze, we were never afterwards able to tell. But as we stood there, the air seemed to shudder and vibrate and the sudden wind that blew around the edges of the door, through the narrow cracks between it and the stone wall, became more violent. For a moment I tried to tell myself that it was a natural phenomenon connected with the sea that must have lain somewhere nearby, on almost the same level as ourselves, and not far beyond the door.

Then, faint but clear, we heard the sound that came from just the other side of the door; a slopping, *oozing* noise which brought the sweat boiling from every pore in my body, which transfixed me to that accursed spot because I knew, although I could not see, *what it was!*

That evil-spawned thing which I had witnessed in my dream surging up from that deep black yonder which heaved and swelled beyond the cliffs, that metamorphic creature whose image stood poised above that time-dimmed, century-stained altar somewhere in the shivering darkness behind us, was a reality; was just beyond that door and trying to get in! Something struck hard on the wood from the other side sending a hollow echo booming into the stillness around the high, rearing walls of the chamber. A few seconds more and our breaths were literally torn from our shaking lips. The metal-studded door quivered and shook visibly under a torrent of blows. Carfax staggered back, almost dropping the lantern in his fright. Pengarden yelled something I could not distinguish. My fear waxed high again and suddenly there came a fresh burst of terror at the sound that proceeded from the other side of the door.

It was indescribable. A croaking, moaning, monstrous whistling sound that grew rapidly in volume until it shrieked fiendishly in our ears and reverberated from wall to wall. Unlike anything I had experienced before, it came to us, malignant and evil, sweeping past us as we turned and fled back up that hideously sloping cavern floor, past that grotesque statue which had now assumed a more sinister and terrifying aspect, up the steep flight of strangely carved steps the significance of which I now thought I knew. Slipping and falling in our terrified haste to get away while behind us, as if mocking our efforts to escape, the thudding, thunderous blows on the wooden door grew into a maniacal fury, unnatural and colossal.

Only God in heaven, if there is such a merciful God, knows how we escaped from that veritable pit of Hell, back into the small cellar and up into the grey daylight which filtered through the narrow windows of the manor.

I should have known the people of the district had a good reason for shunning Faxted Manor as they did; I ought to have known the family who had lived in this place many years before I had come, had never seen the shores of South Africa. What must have really happened to them will probably never be known and the guesses I could have made, probably extremely close to the truth, were of the kind that no one in their sane mind would ever believe.

Far better to say they had simply packed their bags and left them to begin speculating on other reasons for the disappearance. And what of those others who had lived in this accursed place? The demon-cursed family of the Warhopes, steeped in the very evil of which the house reeked? When nothing emerged from those abysmal depths beneath the house, I locked myself in the library going frantically through the incredibly ancient, cobwebbed books on the dusty shelves, knowing that before I finally left Faxted Manor for good, I had to discover the entire truth, even though it might rip the last vestiges of sanity from me.

Pengarden and Carfax had seen and heard enough. Late that morning, in company with Mary Ventnor, they left, preferring to walk to Bude through the storm, which had begun to blow up from the west, rather than remain another hour under that accursed roof. I could not find it in my heart to blame them, nor to try to dissuade them from going. Once or twice in each dark century perhaps, there are unguessable horrors revealed to men, which can be neither understood nor disregarded. This was undoubtedly one of them and I, too, fully intended to leave before nightfall.

There were passages in the books, which now took on another meaning. In the light of what I knew, what I had heard and *almost seen,* I was able to read into the veiled and sometimes deliberately garbled account, the plain and unembellished truth.

It was five o'clock when I finally laid down the last of the books and rose to my feet, going over to the high, narrow window and looking out over the barren moorland at the rear of the house, the weed-choked gardens now full of horrible growths as if nature had regressed, gone back to the ultimate in foulness and degeneracy. Around me, the house was exceptionally quiet. There was not a single creak in the ancient woodwork, even though, outside, the wind, which came howling in from the wild Atlantic, blew and raged around the eaves and angled abutments.

The stillness, the utter stillness, was nerve-rending. My uneasiness grew with every passing minute and it struck me that there was something oppressively furtive about the quietness of the place and when I paused consciously to analyse my thoughts, I found that I was subconsciously waiting for something to happen, something I dreaded but to which I could give no name.

I fell to wondering what Carrington's reaction would be if he knew the full story of this accursed place as I now did. For years, he had been merely scratching around on the surface without getting anywhere near the terrible reality of Faxted Manor. I knew that it must all have originated so many centuries ago that without the books and that terrifying experience down among those tunnels with which the entire rock must have been riddled, it would have been impossible for anyone to get the faintest glimmering of the true facts, the full horror.

There must have been some prehistoric temple on the site in which the most abominable rites had been carried out and later, when the monastery had been built close to the ruins of the carved stone pillars, the old, nameless ceremonies had been carried on until King Edgar in his wisdom, had put to death the perpetrators, razing the monastery to the ground. But the horror was still there, had been wounded but not killed as King Edgar must have fervently hoped, lying dormant in that tunnel-ridden hill with long, slime-bedecked passages leading out to the sea where Charybdis, or some similar heathen monster — for who among us can state that there is only one such foul abomination on this planet — waited, undying, with an insatiable appetite for evil?

Charybdis, or Karyptes, ageless, remembered and feared by the ancient Greeks, but powerful in the long aeons before that time, when mankind was young, worshipped during those terrible, orgiastic rites, coming at intervals out of the sea with others of its kind. Now the elusive records made sense. Now the terror was seen as cold, dark, naked fact. Those unnatural matings between the Warr Hoppes during the Thirteenth and Fourteenth Centuries and, if the documents were anything to go by, continuing almost to the present day.

Nylene Poiseder, the wife of Henry Warhope during the early Sixteenth Century; one of those abominable creatures, an *outsider,* non-human in every respect except perhaps in general outward appearance, theoretically alien, the object of far-spread tales of those days, disturbing stories, which now held for me a more sinister meaning than before. What fearful happenings had occurred then? The hidden heirs of the Warhopes, kept locked away from the light of day and the sight of the peasants, down there in those dripping catacombs under the manor. There would have been some with more man in them than beast; and others so different from man that even the sight of them would have turned men mad. Things like William Warhope, whose body had been discovered on the beach, whose disfigurement had been such that it had been buried with no ceremony and an undue haste in the sand; and as late as 1784, one of the members of the family had been burned on the moors just behind the house and even to this day nothing would grow there. It was as if the ground contained some evil nourishment, which would allow nothing hallowed to flourish.

With an effort, I pulled my thoughts

back to the present. The most merciful thing in this world is the inability of the mind to take in every aspect of any situation and correlate them into a coherent whole. Had mine been able to do so, I would undoubtedly have gone insane at that very instant. But a generous nature had decreed the impossibility of piecing together every little scrap of seemingly disassociated information into the final, sense-obliterating reality.

The events of that morning had faded and become a little blurred in my brain so that by the time the vaguely-seen watery sun had gone down in a clustering of darkening clouds, I refused to let the hazy qualms overtake me and fought them down as I moved through the house, going from one room to the next. But as I reached the main door there came a sudden return of that nameless fear which had all but overwhelmed me in those Stygian depths far beneath the foundations.

I thought I was prepared for the worst and I should have been, considering all that had gone before. Yet when that dreadful clang, harsh and metallic, came from that deep below the house, echoing and reverberating along those terrible passages which honeycombed the cliff, my hands trembled so violently on the handle of the door that for long, precious seconds, I tugged vaguely at it before it opened and I rushed out into the twilight.

The wind, howling like a demonical thing, swirled about me. Because of that abnormal stillness inside the manor, I had temporarily forgotten about the storm, which had come sweeping in across the bay over the grey, heaving waters of the Atlantic. Rain slashed at my face. Moisture, dank and foul, ran among the fungoid weeds and overgrown plants underfoot. Walking or running on that treacherous surface was difficult enough; but I did my best and just before I reached the top of the cliff, I threw a quick look behind me, over my shoulder.

The tall, ancient spires and turrets of Faxted Manor rose at my back, clawing spectrally for the storm-torn heavens where the round, leering face of the leprous moon showed for brief intervals, throwing no light on the scene below. But in the faint, murky greyness and the occasional flash of vivid lightning, there was light enough for me to see by; too much light, for behind me, not close to the manor but down there below where the surf pounded on the rocks, something far less tranquil than those dreaming spires arrested my notice and held me immobile, rooted to the spot.

What I saw down there where the white line of foam crashed on to the grey needles of rock — or what I fancied I saw — was a heart-stopping, disturbing suggestion of movement. The distance was perhaps three hundred feet and for a long second I could discern nothing in detail, but I did not like the look of what I could see.

The things were pale, leprous white, glistening too much in the light of a lightning flash, dripping with water, clawing their way around the tall, black monolith in the small bay, slipping through the water with a horribly, undulant motion. And there was a suggestion of sound, too, audible even above the shrieking voice of the wind — a bestial, *flopping* and a hooting, which could have been emitted by no human throat. These were the things which had made those inhuman marks upon the beach, half-dreamed of monsters from some realm outside of our everyday knowledge and fancies, drawn out of vivid nightmares, whispered of down the long, grey ages, so evil that all reference to their true nature had been deliberately withheld from the eyes of ordinary people. Was it possible that such creatures could have actually been spawned here on Earth, maybe some incredibly old species, probably some strange branch in the tree of evolution? The grain of truth that lay at the very root of the old myths of gods and goddesses? Those mythical beings living during the old times? Those terrible, half-men, half-beast gods of ancient Egypt and, further back in time, of long lost Samaria and Lemuria, of the black stone city of Ib that was old before the first man walked the Earth? From what demonic, blasphemous reality had these ignorant first-people drawn inspiration for the statues and carvings on the walls of the long-dead tombs along the Nile and the Euphrates?

There are those who believe that there is no reality, that these things existed only in the fertile imaginations of the priestly cult seeking power over the mass of the people. And yet I saw them that storm-shrieking night, standing rooted to the spot on that godforsaken, accursed cliff; saw them come leaping, hopping, surging, out of the limitless black deeps of the sea, filing up some half-seen track in an evil, malignant, putrescent stream.

For all of that time I had seen them but dimly, indistinctly, in the heaven-sent darkness. But then, for a long and nightmarish instant, the clouds parted and the flooding yellow moonlight lit the scene almost as bright as day. I saw them clearly then, my mind hovering on the abysmal edge of madness. I think their colour was a greyish-white and in the moonlight they were mostly smooth-skinned or scaly with the suggestion of fins along their backs and the arms and legs were webbed, fibrous, their features repellent with wide-bulging eyes that stared unblinkingly into the night. The first had almost reached the top of the cliffs and still a limitless stream of them was emerging from the sullen swell when something snapped inside my mind. The spell was mercifully broken. I turned and ran headlong into the night. A thin scream rose and fell in my ears, following me, seemed to swell in tune to the rapid thudding of my heart in its frenzied rhythm and long seconds passed before I recognised the inarticulate yelling as my own.

There came a long, sustained peal of thunder, splitting the heavens asunder and close on its heels, like a cavernous roar out of the gaping mouth of Hell itself; a rumbling, grinding, grating sound as the ground shook and shuddered under my feet. Great fissures opened in the rocks. Chasms appeared behind me and in one agonised glimpse, twisting my head with a wrenching of my neck muscles, I saw the front wall of the manor buckle and bulge, twist outward and fall.

It seemed the entire rock-face was crumbling into the sea, carrying with it that blasphemous place. There was a vile, graveyard stench that came out of the ground on every side. Choking and gasping, no longer caring what went on my back, knowing only that I had to get away from that place, while there was still time, I ran with the howling wind, my lungs bursting with the terrible strain, my legs leading and afire with the tremendous effort. The reality of what I had seen was searing through my mind. I could not rid myself of the thought of that spawn of evil which had risen up from the deep and unknown fathoms within the sea, of what lay down in the tunnels beneath the manor itself, tunnels along which the seawater must have been permeating endlessly with the sweeping tides everyday for countless hundreds, thousands, of years, weakening the whole cliff until that night when it had crumbled in upon itself, carrying Faxted Manor with it as it slid into the sea.

In Bude, shortly before midnight, I stumbled into Carrington's room, more dead than alive, babbling a strange and almost incoherent tale. Somehow, with brandy, he managed to pull me round, got something out of me which sent him, ashen-faced, to the telephone.

A small party of men left Bude a little before two o'clock in the morning with the storm abating quickly, made their way out along a narrow path over the rocks and around the headland to Faxted Manor. Carrington had taken care to tell the authorities very little of what I had blurted out to him.

Perhaps it was just as well that he did for there are things hidden just beyond the fringe of human knowledge and experience far best forgotten, even if by some they can never be ignored. The men returned a little after dawn the next day, strangely subdued. They asked questions, firmly put in a kindly tone, went away only partly satisfied by what Carrington and I had agreed to tell them.

Whether it was the action of all that tremendous mass of rock falling into the sea, or whether there are deeper reasons, it was difficult to say, but for days afterwards, the sea was a raging turmoil near that spot and the small fishing vessels, which normally sailed those waters kept well clear of the area. There was, too, an unwholesome smell, which persisted in the region for most of the winter, but by which time I had returned to London, knowing that there could be neither peace nor rest for me in Devon.

The letter I received from Carrington three weeks after my return to Chelsea told me little I had not already guessed, but there was one strange passage in it which struck a responsive of chord of fear in my mind, which is perhaps one of the reasons why the doctors fear I shall never fully recover from my experience.

'There is nothing now recognisable of the place which was known as Faxted Manor since the entire cliff collapsed into the sea at that point. The general opinion is that the action of the salt water on porous rock, riddled with underground passages and vaults was sufficient to cause the entire structure to disintegrate. Be that as it may, I feel

somehow oddly certain that those sub-human creatures you saw did not die. Someday they will inevitably rise again, if not here in Devon, then at some other place, evil and indestructible, ready to seek out and destroy all who know their terrible secret.'

4

Dust

It is fortunately seldom that one experiences such a moment of pure, unadulterated terror as befell me in the autumn of 1936, following a series of inexplicable incidents which, even now, I cannot possibly explain. At the end of June in that year I had relinquished my post as lecturer in mythology and ancient history at Cambridge and accepted the offer of my uncle, James Oliver, to live with him in the large, rambling house on the outskirts of Wisterton, a picturesque fishing village on the Northumberland coast, some fifteen miles from Newcastle. For almost six years I had been working sporadically on my book dealing with the legends of this part of the country, but of late my academic duties had interfered more and more with it and when the opportunity of devoting all my time to it had arisen I had seized it willingly and gratefully.

The thought of actually living in that region of age-old myth and legend had an exhilarating effect on my mind and I experienced a curious sense of excitement as my train rumbled north from York through wild, untouched countryside into deeply-forested places of which I had often read and dreamed, but never visited. This was a primitive part of England where old things were still remembered and the green, domed hills, which nestled low on the skyline hinted of half-forgotten mysteries which had existed there from the very beginning of time. The old tales of Northumberland had their roots deep in misted antiquity and in spite of the speed of the train, it seemed that time had been turned back several centuries as I spied the tiny hamlets set on the low hillsides, clusters of houses gleaming faintly in the late afternoon sunlight.

An increasing and unexplainable atmosphere of elusive alienness seemed to pervade the square, cultivated fields and narrow, winding lanes, half-hidden by tall, thick hedgerows and walls of flint as the train continued further north and the wilderness grew more apparent until it intruded upon my thoughts, giving me the unshakeable feeling that I was an interloper here, that this was a territory I would never be able to understand nor become a part of. Deep gorges and ravines were cut through the dark hills where the sunlight never seemed to penetrate and here and there I caught a glimpse of glinting water as a stream rushed down from the heights to vanish into inconceivable depths.

Certainly there was a strange beauty about the scenery I saw from the carriage window but it was as though an underlying malignancy existed there, just beneath the surface, waiting to engulf those who tried to probe too deeply. For a little while, I began to doubt the wisdom of my move but even as the thought crossed my mind, I told myself that this was surely the kind of atmosphere that was essential for me if I was to complete my book. Where else could I find the necessary inspiration if not in the very heart of legend-haunted Northumberland?

I already knew something of the reputation of this part of the country, had spent long hours among musty tomes, searching through ancient parchments, many written in archaic English, some even in the age-old runes of the early centuries. There were, too, other more tangible remains of this haunted past; the circles of stone pillars which existed on the dark hilltops, lost, drowned towns beneath the sea where, whenever the tides were right, millennia-old bells could be heard ringing beneath the swelling waves. The gigantic black hound with the red, glaring eyes which had been reported at various spots in the county, frightening lonely travellers after dark and in more recent times, that terrible affair at Cornforth Abbey, now a fire-blackened ruin. To most people, these old myths were considered ridiculous, gross distortions of still earlier tales, handed down by word-of-mouth at glowing firesides whenever the winds howled off the moors and the blizzards swept over the bleak domed hills. But the deeper I had delved into them, the more I had become convinced that behind all of these wild fantasies, there lay a germ of truth which, for the most part, lay hidden so far back in time that it might never be revealed. There were old gods here long before the Romans or the invading Danes stepped upon the wild shores and the people in those days worshipped strange beings who have no modern counterparts but who, according to the more superstitious folk, have not died but still exist in deep caverns and in undersea caves well below the low-water mark.

The local train I took from Newcastle, arrived in Wisterton a little after six o'clock and as I walked out of the tiny station into the street, I found several cars drawn up against the curb along with a handful of taxis but nowhere was there any sign of my uncle. Hesitating for only a moment, I was on the point of heading for one of the waiting taxis when a tall, thin-faced man approached me and enquired whether I was Ernest Oliver. After being assured that I was, he explained that my uncle had been detained on urgent business and had asked him to meet me and drive me out to the small village of East Wisterton, which was apparently some five miles from Wisterton. It was, he indicated, a long enough journey and the cost of taking a taxi would indeed be prohibitive.

As we drove out of the town, taking the road along the rugged coast, he explained that he was a business acquaintance of my uncle and that he had already heard a lot about me, even to the point of knowing why I had relinquished my post at the university to come to this desolate spot on the coast. After a long, somewhat tiring train journey I found it distinctly refreshing to be able to sit back and relax and listen to the other as he described several of the landmarks which showed themselves clearly on the skyline to the west. The nearness of the strangely domed hills, topped by thick copses, now intruded more pronouncedly on my consciousness and I realised that I had not been mistaken in my belief that here were strange primal and time-touched things, incredible and alien, which in spite of the late afternoon sunlight, brought a little shiver to my body.

All that I had learned of this county welled up inside me as I stared out of the window of the car, striving to read something into the signs I saw all about me. Here and there, narrow lanes branched off the main road and vanished in leafy mystery on either side, while deep green labyrinths loomed on top of us at every bend in the road. We passed few cars on the way and after fifteen minutes or so, rounding a steep bend, we came within sight of the sea once more, far below us, while in the distance, the sunlight touched the white, spectral finger of a lighthouse standing on a rocky headland thrusting out into the sea.

But as we began the breathtaking descent towards East Wisterton, a tiny cluster of whitewashed houses about a mile distant, I noticed something that attracted my attention oddly, although I could not define the reason for it. Less than a quarter of a mile from the village there stood a two-storey house, which seemed unusually large and elegant for its situation. Even from that distance I could see that it was no longer occupied. There was a general air of stagnation and decay about it that was unmistakable.

Several of the windows appeared to be broken for they did not reflect the sunlight as most of the others did and there was a tantalising air of familiarity about it, which made me feel distinctly uneasy. I knew I had never seen it before, either in real life or in a picture, nor had I heard my uncle speak of it in any of his lectures or on the few occasions when we had met in Cambridge. Yet the feeling that I knew it intimately persisted during the rest of the drive to the village.

My guide dropped me off in front of my uncle's house but made no attempt to alight himself, saying that he still had some urgent business to do in the village and that if my uncle had not yet arrived home, I would be sure to find the door open. I watched as he drove on into the village and then made my way slowly along the carefully-tended path to the house. As the other had said, the front door opened to my touch and I went inside, setting down my two suitcases after receiving no answer to my call.

When my uncle arrived twenty minutes later, I was shocked and surprised at the haggardness of his expression. There were deep purple circles under his eyes and he looked as though he had not slept for several nights. In response to my enquiries he would say little more than that there had been certain odd occurrences in the village over the past few months and in his role of the local doctor he had been helping the police with their investigations. It was with a trace of genuine dread and concern that I tried to question him further for it was utterly out of character for him to take things so seriously, but he refused to go into more detail until we had eaten.

We ate the meal in silence, an uneasy silence which began to eat at my nerves and when we eventually settled down in the easy chairs in front of the fire in the parlour, smoking our pipes, I waited for him to explain the situation with a growing sense of alarm. When he spoke, it was evident he was more overwrought than I had expected.

'To begin with, Ernest, I have a confession to make to you. This dreadful affair has been going on now for more than six months and my main reason for asking you to come and stay with me was not so much to provide you with a place of comparative solitude where you could finish your book in peace and quiet as to provide me with both moral and intellectual support in this hideous matter. Things are pretty bad and I think the climax is near in spite of everything we have been able to do. You have some kind of experience of these nightmare happenings on an indirect, if not direct, level and most of all you will not be inclined to scoff at my ideas, nor are you so steeped in superstition as to be mortally afraid as the rest of the folk are hereabouts. But I must begin at the very beginning. No doubt you noticed the old Carter place on your way here, about a quarter of a mile or so outside the village. It's been empty now for more than five years, just an empty shell of a place since Henry Carter died, but even before we found him stiff and cold at the foot of the stairs there had been a lot of unwholesome talk about the place.'

'What kind of talk?' I asked.

My uncle shrugged, plainly ill at ease. 'The usual sort. Strange blue lights in the windows at night, terrible sounds whenever the moon was full and a frightful odour about the place. It only needs someone to begin a rumour such as that and the place becomes haunted, the home of ghosts and untold horrors even when there is, in all probability, quite a logical and scientific explanation for the happenings. You will probably call what I am going to tell you raving at first, Ernest, but in time, if you decide to stay, you will appreciate that your knowledge is on a totally different plane to that which exists here. Anyway, once Carter was dead, the horror came to East Wisterton with a vengeance. No one from the village would dare to go anywhere near that house, especially after dark. Those of us who had hoped that these idiotic myths concerning the place would die a natural death were doomed to disappointment. If anything, they got worse, much worse. The most disturbing thing had begun some time ago, the complete disappearance of at least six people in as many months. All of these people came from outside the area and you can well imagine a house such as that, with its evil and malodorous reputation, is of a kind to powerfully attract the morbidly curious. There's no direct proof that any of these people did visit this place or that it had any direct connection with their disappearance, but village gossip as it is, we naturally had to be sure. We've searched the place from cellar to attic without finding a trace whatsoever of them; *yet it is an undeniable fact that they have vanished off the face of the Earth*.'

'Maybe they did go there but the general atmosphere was such that they left without giving any indication of their intentions,' I suggested.

He shook his head emphatically. 'We naturally probed that possibility thoroughly. On two occasions, anxious relatives came to enquire about them but without any conclusive results. As a doctor, there was little I could do in an official capacity. There were no bodies on which to conduct a post-mortem, nothing definite at all — until two days ago.'

Pausing at this point, my uncle sucked meditatively on his pipe as if reluctant to continue with his narrative, then slowly and concisely related a story that both frightened and disturbed me, all the more because I had had a vague inkling of it ever since my first sight of this county from the speeding train.

It appeared that two days before, a little after midnight, he had been called urgently to the hospital some three miles inland where an attempted suicide had been brought in suffering from acute shock, together with multiple bruising and abrasions. On arrival, he had examined the patient, shocked to discover that it was a close neighbour of his — a certain Hedley Trelawney — and although his bodily injuries were of a relatively minor nature, it was his mental condition which had given rise to much alarm.

From the local police sergeant, he had learned that two fishermen, making their way along the narrow cliff road, not far from the old Carter house, had been startled to hear hideous screaming coming from the deserted grounds of the place and a few moments later had spotted a dark figure, arms waving madly, race over the cliffs and throw itself off the edge into what would have been a three hundred foot drop on to the needle-shaped rocks below. Hurrying to the scene, they had peered over the edge, fully expecting to see the smashed body lying on the floor below, but as luck would have it, an outjutting branch had caught the man's coat and held him less than twenty feet down the sheer wall of the cliff.

Evidently something unutterably horrible had sent the man running from that accursed place and neither man had any wish to remain in the vicinity, but when no further horror manifested itself, they had plucked up sufficient courage to rescue the unfortunate wretch, clambering precariously over the ledge to where he hung suspended on that slender branch, which was all that lay between him and a mangled death below. Working desperately, they had finally succeeded in getting him to the top where he had screamed and struggled furiously so that it had taken all of their combined strength to subdue him and carry him to the nearest cottage where they had then driven him to the hospital, recognising this as a case which my uncle would not be able to handle alone.

Although Trelawney had been given a powerful sedative on admittance, he still appeared to be partially conscious and it was his rambling mutterings that had frightened two of the nurses and prompted the hospital doctor to call my uncle in the hope that he might be able to throw some light on the matter. As far as he had been able to make out from the almost unintelligible mouthings, the words that Trelawney kept repeating over and over again were:

'Knew he weren't dead: none of that accursed family ever did really die. Grey dust . . . everywhere! A thousand different shapes . . . spinning . . . the vortex . . . all dust, grey and blue-crimson. Carter must have found out the way to call it up . . . fed it on the others. God! All that dust . . . spinning . . . '

Trelawney was still under restraint and continual observation at the hospital and the doctors there were doubtful if his mind would ever be right again. There seemed no doubt that he had seen something in that house, something so fearful that his mind had snapped under the terrible mental strain. My uncle would have liked to have questioned him further, for he felt certain now that there were things which he ought to know; but it had become increasingly obvious that it would be a very long time, if ever, before Trelawney would speak sensibly and coherently again.

My first impulse was to suggest that these had been nothing more than the ravings of delirium but I knew that this must already have occurred to my uncle, who was in a far better position to judge than I was, so I did not put my initial thoughts into words but sat silent, shivering a little in spite of the warmth of fire in the wide hearth. What my uncle had now revealed to me hinted at darker, more malignant, forces existing here than I had ever read or dreamed of, although in some of the forbidden volumes I had perused there had been the passages which had hinted at monstrous things, not of Earth, which had at one time inhabited this planet and which might still do so though now hidden behind myth and legend following the encroachment of civilisation and scientific discovery.

Plainly there was the possibility that this might be just such a thing and sitting there in that quiet parlour, I found nothing absurd about it. For the rest of the evening and well into the early hours of the morning, we discussed the situation as calmly as we could, trying to decide what to do about this outburst of terror that had descended upon the village. It seemed acutely uncanny even in a part of the country where strange and often frightful things were commonplace. From my uncle's description, it was clear that nothing would be gained by further questioning of the central figure in the drama — Trelawney himself — and whatever we did, it would have to be done by ourselves. In quite a short time, we had reached the conclusion that the only way to satisfy ourselves would be to stay for a night in the Carter house, to discover at first hand what untold horror had sent Trelawney screaming wildly from the place to throw himself off the cliff in an effort to end his fear-crazed life, an attempt which only a blind and merciful providence had foiled.

Accordingly, we resolved in our minds on the best course to take; which weapons we should take with us in order to protect ourselves against any contingency and how to track down this blasphemous nightmare which had, if we had read the signs correctly, been responsible for the disappearances of six people and the near suicide of another. When we finally ended our discussion, it was almost four o'clock and as I made my way upstairs to my room, it was with a feeling of oppressive fear mingled with a sense of growing excitement.

I undressed quickly for I was very tired and my brain was reeling with a chaos of half-formed thoughts and ideas, some idiotic, others making a little more sense and I could not escape the sense of dread and impending disaster as I thought of that terrible and lonely place out there on the edge of the cliffs. Was it possible that there, in this wild, isolated region there lurked nightmare, supernatural forces such as are undreamed of by present-day science, denied by the church, and come only in dreams to a few sensitive people?

Switching off the light, I stood by the window for a moment, looking out into the star-strewn night. The sea was a dark shadow on the edge of the land and the muted thunder of the surf was a pleasant, normal sound in my ears. There were no lights showing in the village and the houses were dark, squat shapes lying silent in the vague, dim starlight.

Instinctively, almost, I glanced in the direction of the Carter house, just visible as I craned my head forward until my forehead touched the cold glass of the window.

I had no wish to gaze long upon it for I wanted to sleep, but the tales that my uncle had told me tormented my restless mind. I had expected to see it looming there, a grotesque shadow, standing high on the cliff edge, dark and empty and full of malevolent, blasphemous influences. What I did see, however, was something vastly different, something soul-destroying and so utterly unexpected that I did not know whether I was awake or dreaming. Surely nothing sane and normal could have caused that weirdly flickering bluish-crimson glow that shone forth from every window, through each broken pane of glass in that accursed house. The rambling tale told by those two fishermen who had watched Trelawney run from the place came rushing back into my confused mind. A practical joker, someone playing on the simple, superstitious villagers? Or something of a far darker and sinister nature? Desperately, I attempted to pull my scattered thoughts together, stop my hands from shaking convulsively where they gripped the window ledge until all the blood had left them and there remained no feeling at all in my fingers. As I watched, unable to move a single muscle, unable to think coherently, that monstrous glow waxed brighter until it seemed to form overlapping shells surrounding that ghastly house on the cliff.

Whether that vision was a reality or born of illusion, I shall never really know, nor how long I stood there shivering from a mixture of cold and utter fear. I must have staggered back to my bed and fallen upon it in a semi-conscious state for when I finally awoke, I was lying on top of the sheets, my limbs icily cold and the bright early morning sunshine shining in through the window onto my face.

My first decision was to inform my uncle of what I had seen but in broad daylight everything seemed as ephemeral as a bad dream and I put it down to an overwrought imagination, keeping my fears to myself. Thus it was that we spent the day making all possible preparations for the coming night. We would take loaded revolvers with us, although neither of us believed that these forces, whatever their true nature, could be defeated by bullets. In addition, we had powerful torches and a portable recording machine with which we hoped to capture on waxen cylinders any strange sounds that might manifest themselves. My uncle had also procured a large plate camera and tripod, equipped with powerful flashbulbs with which to photograph any visual apparitions.

All of this took us several hours but by mid-afternoon everything was in readiness. In order to learn as much as possible of what we might expect to find, I spent some hours in my uncle's well-stocked library, going through old reports appertaining to the Carter house, seeking some clue which might aid us in our search for the horror which was reputed to lurk there. Here, I was surprised to find several volumes of ancient folklore concerning the district and other dusty manuscripts, which shed a terrible light on the region, yielding information that brought a shudder of dread to me. Terror had lived in this wild region for more than half a millennium. There were records of a certain William Stanthorpe, who had been dragged from the village in the June of 1586 and burned on the hill overlooking the cliffs, accused of calling the Devil himself out of the air and of bringing a terrible blight to the village and the surrounding countryside.

Going even further back in time, one chronicle spoke of a nightmare happening in 1417 when unwary travellers along the coastal road were snatched from their horses by a terrible, whirling shape and carried off in the direction of the old mansion perched high on the cliffs — my reading soon confirmed that this mansion had stood on the very spot where the Carter house had later been built in the nineteenth century. Many of the tales were of a deliberately vague nature, merely hinting at fearsome, obscene occurrences, of demons which inhabited the area and which could be called into existence by those who knew the correct formulae and incantations, who knew just when the signs were right and who *fed* these creatures on the right kind of sustenance. It was this last phrase that brought a wave of nausea into my stomach and the sweat popping out on my forehead and along the small of my back. Evidently the horror that now held East Wisterton in its grip was of no recent occurrence. It had been there for five hundred years, half-forgotten, it is true, but lurking just below the surface of everyday life like some malignant growth, biding its time, waiting once more, *until the signs were right,* and someone came along who knew the words which could bring it into being again to terrorise the neighbourhood. I could see now why the police were forced to confess themselves baffled by the disappearances of those six men during the past few months, why my uncle did not dare to confess his private fears to anyone but myself, for who apart from the naturally superstitious villagers would listen to him, let alone believe him?

As evening approached, so did my inherent dread increase and by the time the sun went down in a flaring of red and gold over the hills, I could scarcely contain my fear. Had it been possible to think up some excuse for not accompanying my uncle on this nocturnal mission — for he, it seemed, had already made up his mind to go through with it — I would have seized it gratefully. As it was, I knew I had now irrevocably committed myself and it was with a sense of acute trepidation that I piled our apparatus into the back of his battered old car and clambered into the seat beside him.

We did not indulge in conversation during the short drive along the cliffs for each of us was engrossed in his own private thoughts. As I have said, my uncle, in company with the police, had searched the old house from top to bottom on two occasions without finding any trace of anything out of the ordinary.

On the face of things, this was exactly what we found as we pushed open the creaking outer door and manhandled the items of our equipment inside. There was still sufficient light streaming in through the smashed windows by which to make out details of the interior of the house and my first incredulous impression was of white dust which lay over everything, covering the floor to a depth of almost an inch. The main chamber of the lower floor was extremely large, measuring almost twenty-five feet along each wall, with a wide, double-window which looked out on to the overgrown lawn sweeping down to the edge of the narrow road bordering the cliffs. It must have been across that rough, knee-deep grass that Trelawney had run, screaming aloud his fear three nights before. For several minutes we busied ourselves in setting up the recording machine and the camera on its heavy tripod, fitting one of the flashbulbs in place ready for instant use.

Not until this was done were we able to relax and look about us and almost at once, now that the work of preparation was over, I was struck by the air of malignancy which hung over the house, an atmosphere which stirred me strongly. Most vivid of all was the thick carpet of dust and it was abundantly clear that Trelawney had not been imagining this in his wild ravings at the hospital. There was a shifting hint of untold terror here, exemplified by the thick dust underfoot, dust, which could not ordinarily have gathered in anything less than a thousand years of slow accumulation. The place disturbed me curiously and to say that I was prepared to see anything there is a gross understatement. We settled ourselves down in front of the wide window where, in spite of the faint draft, which came in through the shattered panes, we felt relatively secure. We had no means of knowing from which direction danger might come, but here, at least, we had two avenues of escape, back into the house or out through the weed-tangled grounds.

As it grew darker, the air of menace became stronger. There were no lights in the house and we were loath to use our torches until it was absolutely necessary. It was our idea to switch on the recording machine the moment we heard anything abnormal and then stand by the camera which had been set up at the entrance to the large chamber so that it was possible to swivel it on its tripod to cover the room, the long passages outside and the wide, spiral stairway which led upstairs.

So far, we had noticed nothing visually unnatural in spite of the abnormality of the atmosphere in that large chamber, but as my uncle walked up and down before the window I saw something that brought a fresh rush of noxious horror to me so that I cried out aloud. There was not a strong light shining through the windows now. The pale rays of the setting moon, near its first quarter, gave just sufficient light to cast a leprous radiance upon the floor of that accursed room and the perspiration broke out on my forehead as I saw my uncle's footprints in the greyish-white dust were slowly being obliterated, *smoothed out of existence as the dust, moving of its own volition, with a hideous life all of its own, flowed back into place, erasing them completely!*

At the same time, even as the shock of this discovery was numbing our minds, a fresh horror attracted our attention. For a moment, it merely appeared as though the pale moonlight was waxing stronger, lighting the room with an unhealthy glow and a chill of unutterable fear settled on us as we saw that this was no natural yellow glimmer such as might be cast by the moon, but was something far more monstrous and — *familiar.* It was that hell-born, blue-crimson glow I had seen the night before and which had been visible over the house shortly before Trelawney had attempted to hurl himself to his death over the cliff edge.

My mind, as sharp and alert as my senses, recognised the danger instantly. With a wild cry of warning, I leapt to my feet and ran towards the camera, intending to gain a permanent record of this horror but before I could reach it, there came such a scream of malignant, mocking triumph from the top of the wide stairs that I fell back as though struck by a physical blow. As I lifted my head to peer into the dim shadows, lit by that weird, evil glare which flared and writhed in cocoons of cold flame, I dreaded what I was to see. A wild desire to turn and flee from that place seized me so strongly that it needed all of my courage to fight it down and stand my ground. I sensed my uncle moving close behind me, could hear his harsh, irregular breathing, felt his grip tighten on my arm. There was a sudden ghastly stench filling my nostrils and then, horror of horrors — out of the floor at the top of the stairs, there rose a monstrous spinning column of dust, a damnable hideousness which defied all human comprehension, bubbling and surging out of some hellish realm of untold blasphemy. From what far void that thing came, by what madness unknown to the laws of nature and science as we are aware of them it was able to take on shape and substance, I shall never know. My brain was a shrieking chaos as I stood rooted to the spot, watching that fearsome apparition move towards me, changing form as it approached. It bore no human resemblance although there were eyes as Trelawney had muttered in his delirium; hellish, red eyes that flickered with a rapacious greed beyond life.

Dimly, I was aware of my uncle stumbling forward, his face working horribly, the contorted features mouthing and writhing as though he was struggling to mutter some of the odd incantations we had found in those forbidden tomes locked away in his library. As he reached the foot of the stairs, barely twenty feet from that accursed thing, a few disjointed fragments came to me above the roaring of the blood in my ears. He was not, as I had first thought, speaking in English. Indeed, as I now remember, in retrospect, the words were in no language I had ever heard spoken before, mad phrases drawn out of the nightmare beginnings of mankind.

There seemed to come a halt in the descent of that whirling, gyrating column. Putrid, shimmering, unutterably alien and evil, it hovered there in that fiendish crimson glare, gigantic and hostile, and then the final culmination of our vigil, the most apocalyptic horror of all. Inwardly, I had somehow steeled myself to meet all that might transpire, even this abysmal fiend from the bottomless pit of cosmic, gibbering lunacy, but what happened next sent me staggering, screaming, back into the room, my shaking fingers clutching frantically at the door posts for support. For even as my uncle moved forward, thrusting himself towards the bottom of the stairs, as though fighting his way against some terrible, invisible force, a rope-like tendril of animated dust, directed by some fiendish intelligence, swept down, caught him around the middle and plucked him off his feet, carrying him through the air, finally smashing his helpless form down onto the wide landing at the top of the stairs.

As I crouched against the bottom of the door, shivering uncontrollably, fingernails scrambling insanely at the wooden panels, I tried to shut my eyes to the sight of what was happening there, tried to close my ears to the terrifying screams which rent the air and hammered on my seething brain. The frightful stench had all but overpowered me, my breath became stopped in my constricted throat. But my resolution failed me. It was impossible to keep my eyes shut at the sight of that ghastly spectacle. Some little germ of reason told me that this was nothing more than a hideous, nightmarish illusion, a figment of my terror-stricken brain.

The shrieks swelled to an indescribable babble of sound and other noises were superimposed on the screams of my poor uncle as the dust all about him humped and writhed, flowing over his prone body, clogging eyes and ears and nose, choking his lungs with every shuddering, gasping breath he took.

Who can be sure of what actually takes place under such circumstances as these? I saw that whirling column pause then move as though sightlessly, yet with a terrible singleness of design, drifting in my direction. I have tried to hint at my feelings during those fearful moments although even now I cannot be certain what was fact and what was sheer fantasy. Madly, I stumbled back, my legs quivering under me, unable to tear my gaze away from that horrendous, soul-destroying demon. Vaguely, I remember emptying all six chambers of the revolver at it, then flinging the empty, useless weapon away. That my uncle was dead, or nearly so, I did not doubt and I knew that the same fate awaited me unless I could get away from that terrible place. Arms held in front of me, I retreated towards the windows that looked out upon the grounds and in doing so, my shoulder caught some obstruction immediately at my back. What occurred next was so sudden, so startlingly unexpected, that I could scarcely take it in.

There came an explosive crack, a vivid blinding flash of actinic light that blinded me temporarily; and close on its heels a demonical roar of sheer fury which drowned out every other sound. When I could see again, there was only the diabolical carpet of grey dust on the floor and on the stairs and at the very top of the stairway something virtually unrecognisable that crawled and moaned and tried to stand upright.

Shrieking madly, I turned and ran, half-falling through the broken panes of the windows. Madly, I knew what must have happened. In my clumsiness I had ignited the flashbulb on the camera and that savage, eye-searing glare had somehow been sufficient to stop that monstrosity intent on my destruction.

But coherent thought did not come until much later. What blind instinct guided me through the clinging fungus-like growths, past skeletal-armed trees that writhed and clawed at the star-ridden sky, I do not know. Somehow, I reached the car parked by the side of the narrow lane, dropped into the seat behind the wheel and drove back into the village where I aroused the local police sergeant with my frenzied hammering on his door. My distraught condition and the oddly rambling tale that I managed to stammer out prompted quick action on his part. Within ten minutes he had gathered together a small party of men and although I dreaded what I knew I might see, I agreed to lead them back to that accursed house on the cliff.

There is no doubt now in my mind of the identity of that nameless horror I encountered in the Carter place. Since that terrible night I have spent many hours going through my uncle's books, gathering the scattered clues together into a mad and terrifying whole. The old legends, distorted perhaps over the centuries, were still very close to the truth. The dark, malignant entities from the primaeval chaos, had come to Earth long before the first men had evolved. They were old when the pyramids were young and the first Sumerian tablets still wet clay. Fortunately, they manifested themselves only to an unlucky few throughout the whole of the long millennia, but these occasional brushes with humanity were enough to bring into being the loathsome faiths that have existed since the beginnings of civilisation. There had been long, ageless aeons when they had ruled supreme on Earth and those who knew of them both dreaded and worshipped them.

This, I knew, was one of these elder things, deathless and utterly opposed to men whom they regarded as interlopers on the planet. To their chosen few they made their plans and wishes known in apocryphal dreams and visions while they waited in the dark and hidden places for the time when, as the books all said, the signs would be right and they would take over the world for themselves once more.

During that frantic, nightmare drive back to the village and the return journey to that house on the cliffs, I had found myself wishing with a terrible intensity that we would find nothing there. My uncle, I believed, was dead and gone into realms I could not even imagine, as had at least six poor devils within the memory of the people still living in the village and had it remained that way, I might have somehow found it possible to force my mind to ignore, to forget, that hideous abomination I thought I had seen.

Yet after all, the supreme horror was still to come and the fact that it was witnessed not only by myself, but by the six stalwart and unimaginative men who accompanied me back to the house, means that never again shall I be able to sleep peacefully in my bed, or stand in the faintly shimmering starlight of a summer's night and feel easy in my mind. Perhaps Trelawney is the lucky one, living in a blank emptiness, staring at the walls of the small room in which he is kept at the Newcastle Mental Hospital since his mind has now retreated behind a mental barrier through which nothing can penetrate.

I will try to set down as concisely and accurately as possible what confronted us as we entered that lower chamber, through the splintered doorway with its sagging lintel and mouldering boards, but here I must choose my words carefully. The men had all brought powerful torches with them and in their combined light the undisturbed grey dust threw back a malevolent glimmer that brought the uncontrolled shivering back into my body. The camera and tripod lay smashed on the floor where I had knocked them over in my heedless fight. My empty revolver lay half-buried in the dust at the bottom of the stairs. In the muffling silence nothing moved as I opened my mouth to call my uncle's name, I thought that perhaps I had imagined or dreamed it all.

But even before I could call, one of the men cried out, pointed a shaking arm and as one man we turned and stared at the unnameable horror that was slowly coming down the stairs to meet us. In the torchlight, the shape and features were barely recognisable, yet we all knew who — *or rather what* — it was!

Only a bubbling, inarticulate sound came through the lips of that which had once been James Oliver, my revered uncle and, even as it crawled, the limbs crumbled into a grey dust, the body collapsing and sagging hideously, *flowing* as it swayed and slithered forward. For a moment, I thought I saw the eyes turned with a look of hopeless pleading in my direction, thought it tried to lift itself upright as a man should walk, but on feet that were no longer flesh and blood, but something infinitely horrible. Then it dropped, dripping into a powder, which had neither shape nor form, joining its substance irretrievably with the rest of the dust that lay thickly over the floors and stairs.

5

The Keeper of Dark Point

There was a thick, white sea mist obscuring the edges of the hills that morning when I stepped down from the ancient coach which had brought me along the endless, twisting roads to this godforsaken spot on the South Devon coast. The muscles of my legs and body were stiff from the long, overnight journey on the train from London and the shorter, though equally wearying ride on the bus, which had brought me south from Kingsbridge. The sleep which I had missed lay heavy behind my eyes and the impact of that first glimpse of the country that lay before me struck me with the force of a physical blow, and although there may have been a sun somewhere beyond that thick veil of darkening fog which hung heavy and impenetrable over the shoreline, the chill of the night and darkness still touched me, still hung in the air and I shivered as I drew in my first breaths of it.

Standing there, listening to the wheezy rattle of the bus as it began to move away from me between the dew-gleaming hedgerows, I felt oddly bewildered and out of place. I had entered this unfamiliar landscape too abruptly for me to be able to take it all in at once. Indeed, as the sound of the bus faded into the muffling distance, I felt a sudden urge to run after it, to climb back on board and leave this place. It was an overpowering impulse and now, looking back over the events that had led up to my being there, I am certain there was some strange foreboding of evil, some presentiment that had something oddly prophetic about it. The bus had vanished around a bend in the road, the groan of its engine fading swiftly into silence and the opportunity was gone.

Not that I recognised it then as an opportunity. As I began to trudge along the road, I felt a sense of surprise at myself and there was a morbid fascination that was disturbing, something I found difficult to analyse or classify. At first, I decided that it was the unworldly aspect of that stretch of rugged coastline, seen at intervals through the writhing tendrils of mist, which brought the feeling of alarm to my mind, and made me uneasy. And then I recollected the letter, which reposed in my breast pocket, the prime reason for my being there and I knew that my uneasiness had a secondary and possibly more potent cause.

Somewhere in this desolate part of the country, I hoped to discover what had happened to my brother. It was almost six months since I had heard anything from him. When he had first come to Devon, two years before, he had written every month, his letters filled with news of ancient folklore of the place, the old legends and myths which he had been investigating for the book he was writing. Then, abruptly, and without any warning whatsoever, all word had ceased. My letters to him had gone unanswered and in the end, I had grown so concerned that I had put an advertisement in the local newspapers asking for any information as to his whereabouts.

Even then, several weeks had passed before I had received a reply, in the shape of the letter that brought me hurrying to Devon by the first train, for there was something about it that had alarmed me intensely. It was not so much that my correspondent had written, as what he had implied in half-veiled tones that had aroused me to my present state of uneasiness.

Taking it out of my pocket, I read it through again, striving to see in that rough, oddly archaic scrawl, the reason for the stirring of fear in my mind:

Traganmawes,
Tor Mount,
South Devon.
William S. Meredith, Esq.
12 St. Mary's Court,
London S.E.1.
September 23, 1934.

My Dear Sir,

Your advertisement asking for details

of the whereabouts of Philip Meredith appeared recently in the Tor Mount Gazette. I believe I am in a position to supply you with news of him which I am sure will prove of interest. I might say that since he came here two years ago, he has been engaged in a study of the most peculiar type, one that has aroused a definite antagonism towards him on the part of the more superstitious people in the neighbourhood. As you may imagine, there are many old legends whispered in this part of the world, queer tales one hears from the local farmers and fisherfolk.

I am afraid your brother was a little too persistent in tracking down the sources of these myths, came a little too close to the truth for his own good. There are things which I cannot put down on paper, and for this reason it is essential you should come here with all speed so that we may meet and discuss the matter.

As for myself, I have both seen and heard things in the hills and in particular in the area near Dark Point, *which appears to be the focal point for most of these manifestations. I suppose all of this will seem strange to a city man, but I must point out that here we see things far differently to most, as you may find if you decide to come. There is a bus that connects with the overnight train to Plymouth at Kingsbridge, getting you here early in the morning. If I cannot meet you, my house is at the far end of the street overlooking the cliffs, some distance from the others and almost halfway towards Dark Point lighthouse.*

Yours very sincerely,
Hedley Lindennan.

My feelings concerning the contents of this letter were not such as to ease the disturbing uneasiness in my mind. I did not, for one moment, believe that there was anything real or sinister in the odd happenings which Lindennan mentioned in such obviously veiled terms, but the fact that he had somehow omitted to give any details as to what had happened to Philip was sufficient to arouse the utmost apprehension in my being. Now, as I made my way through the shrouding mist, I felt a strange sense of fright mingled with the nearness to malevolent and forbidden things and it was easy for me to recognise how unhallowed superstitions might grow out of all proportion in a place such as this. Old beliefs would die hard here, shut away from the tempering effects of the outside world. Perhaps, after all, there were oddly inexplicable happenings taking place in this part of the country, which could have been magnified until they had assumed a dominant role in the lives of these simple-minded people.

Occasionally, as the wind freshened in gusts from the sea, the wall of ocean fog thinned and gave me brief, tantalising glimpses of the village which lay a few hundred yards ahead of me, the solitary road winding through it before it went sharply inland and vanished over the brow of a beetling hill to my right and there, perhaps a mile distant, the white, spectral tower of a lighthouse standing lonely and desolate on a narrow peninsula of rock thrusting out into the beating surf. This, no doubt, was Dark Point.

The village was obviously of wide extent in spite of the small number of dwellings since it stretched in a single line of cottages along the seafront; but here and there, I noticed a deserted and decayed building, mouldering in the mist, a sagging thatched roof, walls crumbling in amid a shamble of wood and bricks in overgrown gardens. It was not a sight calculated to ease the growing apprehension in my mind. Set a little to the rear of the street, just showing above the roofs, I observed the spire of a small church and halfway through the village, a small jetty thrust its way into the sea with a handful of fishing boats drawn up alongside it.

I met no one on the road and there was only the sound of my own footsteps in the muffling mist to keep me company as I passed the sightless, staring windows. This was a place in which I did not care to linger and I was glad when I finally came in sight of the solitary house set a little back from the road, the only one which showed any sign at all of human habitation, a thin wisp of smoke curling from the single chimney.

It was easy to understand why few outsiders ever came to Tor Mount, for unlike most other tiny fishing villages of the South Devon coast it appeared to shut itself away from prying eyes, to shun visitors and there was no air of welcome about the place, although at the time I put it down to the early hour of the morning and the abominable weather conditions.

Hedley Lindennan was a man in his early sixties, evidently well-educated, who greeted me courteously and seemed curiously pleased to see me. He lived alone, but insisted on preparing a meal, waiting until I had eaten before explaining his reasons for asking me to come.

Then, sitting in the comfortable chair in front of the fire — for the morning was still cold for this time of year, I heard the story of Tor Mount and in particular of the Keeper of Dark Point, and as the story unfolded, I knew that my fears concerning the place had not been ill-founded, and I found myself shivering incessantly in spite of the clammy heat in the room. Often, I found it almost impossible to believe certain parts of his narrative for my mind told me that in this day and age such events could not happen, had no place in this sane, everyday world of the Twentieth Century.

When Lindennan had finished I did not wonder that people shunned Tor Mount, nor that the fisherfolk preferred to shut themselves away from the outside world for if there should be even the tiniest grain of truth in that fantastic, horrifying tale, it would be more than enough to explain the air of utter desolation and decay over the village, the mouldering houses and the weed-choked gardens.

There had been many legends and whispered tales in myth-haunted Tor Mount for several centuries, Lindennan said, stemming originally from the ruined village of Torsands which had once flourished, more than five hundred years before and half a mile from Lindennan's cottage, closer to where Dark Point now loomed on its rocky promontory. In spite of its small size, it had been a wealthy place in those days with the sea abounding in fish and crab. Then tragedy had struck at Torsands. The supply of fish dwindled, the boats returned day after day with empty nets and pots and according to the legend, certain evil and shocking practices took place in the village after that. The stories were, as always, deliberately vague and misleading as to the exact nature of these rites, but the terrible outcome of them was sufficiently well established and authenticated. One wild, storm-filled night, so Lindennan understood from his reading of certain old books and documents, a large group of the villagers made their way up to the strange circle of stones on top of High Tor where the Devil held court and here, in the midst of lightning and thunder, the most diabolical scenes were enacted. The tales told of wild sounds, screechings and snarlings, bestial grunts and hideous barkings such as could have been uttered by no human throat and a stench like that from the deeps of the most abominable pit of Hell.

Before dawn the next day, a great wave, sweeping in from somewhere far out in the Atlantic overwhelmed Torsands completely, wiping the place clean of any life which had existed there, shattering the buildings, smashing the boats drawn alongside the quay, destroying everything in a cataclysmic fury that surpassed anything ever previously known. Now, all that remained were empty shells of houses, mounds of shattered stones and the ruined spire of the church, which had earlier been the very centre of these heathen ceremonies.

Ever since that time, there had been reports at irregular intervals of odd things happening in the area. Curious inhuman marks found on the sand at low tide, hideous flopping sounds heard at dead of night when the evil stars shone from the clear, moonless vault of the heavens, misshapen shadows glimpsed from the road by the keepers of the light whenever they made their way along the cliffs to Dark Point from Tor Mount.

There was, too, Lindennan had heard,

a book filled with unknown ideographic symbols which had some bearing on this mad period of the region's history and throughout the intervening centuries, the more superstitious people of the village spoke in hushed tones of flickering lights seen on top of High Tor and mad sounds issuing from that circle of half-ruined stones.

Philip had learned of the existence of this strange book shortly after his arrival in Tor Mount and has spent much of his time searching for it, determined to interpret the weird symbols it contained, confident that it would tell him all he wanted to know of the curious past history of the place, especially of the ruined village of Torsands, which fascinated him unutterably.

He had taken to wandering among the shunned spots, especially after dark, although he had been warned on countless occasions, both by Lindennan and others, to stay away from such shadow-haunted places. The villagers appeared to be sullenly banded together against the intrusion of strangers whom they regarded with both suspicion and dislike. Some strangers, Lindennan hinted, had already vanished mysteriously long before Philip had arrived in Tor Mount, but for a time, although most people outwardly shunned him, no active action had been taken against him. He had bought one of the decaying houses along the front and there had been intense speculation about his doings, particularly the long hours after dark when he would return from his nocturnal wanderings and a solitary light would burn in one window of the cottage until almost dawn.

On May fifteenth — Lindennan recalled the date well since there had been a tremendous storm later that night — my brother had been seen by several people making his way down from the summit of High Tor where he had been spending more and more of his time striving to interpret the crudely hewn hieroglyphics carved on the oddly angled stones, but instead of taking the road down the hill to the village as he usually did he had abruptly turned and made his way along the beetling brow of the hill towards the spectral tower of Dark Point lighthouse.

In answer to my questions, Lindennan confirmed that the lighthouse had been abandoned for close on seventy years following the building of a new tower some three miles along the coast. Apparently, the rocky promontory on which Dark Point was situated had become riddled by subterranean clefts and shafts by the prolonged action of the sea and the foundations were so insecure that the entire structure was in danger of collapse.

Lindennan himself felt certain that Philip had reached the lighthouse before the storm had broken. It was less than three-quarters of a mile from the top of High Tor cut down to the crumbling ruins of the tower, but what had happened then no one could say, although several rumours were rife. For the first time in more than three months no light was seen in the cottage on the edge of the village that night, but with the storm raging over the headland and the lightning flashing and forking across the cloud-scudded heavens, little notice had been taken of this. It was not until three days later when nothing further had been seen of him that anyone decided to go up to Dark Point and see for themselves whether there was any sign of him there.

Hedley Lindennan had been among the party and he could therefore speak from first-hand knowledge of the black horror that had preceded them. Some of the terror of that visit communicated itself to me in the hushed, whispered voice of my host. The sheer bulk of the lighthouse had had an oppressive effect on the small group of men and at first none had dared enter that haunt of dark and shadow, yet there was some irresistible lure about the place, which had a profound effect on them. The main door was locked and barred by massive lengths of wood, securely nailed down but on the seaward side, a yawning aperture in the crumbling stone afforded them entry. Over everything lay an inch-deep shroud of dust faintly lit by the pale light filtering in through the gaping opening. Cautiously, they let themselves in, Lindennan in the lead. There was little to be seen on the ground floor beyond some indistinct marks in the dust, but as they made their way up the steps to the living quarters they received a positive shock of objective horror. Two of the men cried out inarticulately and attempted to cover their eyes. Only Lindennan managed to retain sufficient of his mental and physical composure to go forward, something rendered more difficult since he was in the lead and came upon it first.

There were strange markings around the vast, circular stone walls, very similar to those on the graven black stones atop High Tor, and other blasphemous designs etched on the floor itself — and set in the very centre of the room a tall pillar of octahedral cross-section, on the top of which reposed a hideously carved figure made from an odd kind of stone which had a peculiarly soapy feel.

My host's voice trembled as he attempted to describe that monstrosity. It was, he claimed, like nothing he had ever seen before, something quite outside of his previous experience; a nightmare creation resembling some form of anthropological impossibility which could, in Lindennan's opinion, never have existed in real life. Yet even this faded into insignificance beside what they found on the dusty floor behind the stone column. There were bones there, half-covered in the fine white dust; some evidently human, but others which completely baffled and frightened the men, bearing no resemblance to any creature known, nightmarish things spawned in outer darkness. All of the skeletons were of an incredible age. Lindennan firmly believed they were at least three or four hundred years old, dating back to the time before the great tidal wave that had swept in from somewhere far out in the ocean and engulfed Torsands and the surrounding area.

Here, there were definite signs of someone having been in the tower recently. A few of the bones had clearly been moved as if someone had bent to examine them more closely and the dust on the steps leading up to the very top of the lighthouse had been disturbed although the prints were not easy to define.

I questioned Lindennan more closely on this point, struggling to hide my fear and apprehension concerning his discoveries. In answer to my questions, he replied that he felt certain the footsteps had been made by my brother as no one else in the village would have dared to go out to Dark Point alone. But even while he was talking, it was evident that there was more to come, that the small party from Tor Mount had found more in that dreadful and accursed place and he was having some difficulty in getting to the point.

Remaining together, they had searched the Dark Point lighthouse thoroughly with the exception of the room at the very top. There had been a mouldering wooden trapdoor at the extreme top of the splintered stairs, but as they had stood there in a tiny, huddled group debating whether to go any further and complete their investigations of the place, they had become aware of the frightful fishy odour coming from above and several of the men had fancied they had heard a faint movement from beyond the trapdoor. Afterwards, they had been unable to describe exactly what they thought they had heard. Some considered it to have been a sliding, scraping sound as though a heavy body was being dragged across the floor; others thought it had been a slopping sound almost as if some semi-liquid body had fallen onto the upper floor. Lindennan was of the opinion that it had been nothing more than the wind howling through gaps in the upper structure, putting no supernatural context on it whatever. Nevertheless, the fact remained that no one had ventured into that topmost room.

Something more than fright had now come over all of the explorers in that terrible tower of crumbling stone. Each man would undoubtedly have turned and fled had it not been that he feared the scorn of his neighbours and all were relieved when they finally moved out into the open again to search the ground around the base of the rocks. Even here, horror hung broodingly over everything for they saw in the smooth sand, left by the low tide, there were faint prints leading down to the water. One set was clearly identified as human, made by size eight or nine boots — my brother took size nine — the others were pure undiluted horror. As the men examined them in the pale sunlight, they shuddered visibly, for even though the tide had partially obliterated them there was an obviously unnatural look about them. Huge rounded prints with a set of deeper marks around the edges as if they had been made by a curiously shaped sucker rather than feet and, according to Lindennan, there were too many to have been made by anything walking on *two feet!*

Something had lumbered or slithered across the sand, something mountainous and monstrous, which had walked clear into the sea. Whether it had returned from the water, none of the men could ascertain with any degree of certainty but one thing they were all sure: *those human prints led only one way!*

* * *

It would not be easy to describe the mood in which I was left by these revelations — grotesque and terrifying, I could no longer doubt that those prints in the sand and in the dust of Dark Point lighthouse had been made by my brother — and when Lindennan insisted I should stay with him, rather than at the solitary inn in the village, I readily agreed. From what little I had seen of the village and its other inhabitants, I doubted if I would find ease or comfort there.

During the day, I questioned my host more fully concerning the ancient legends of the place. By now, I was certain that if I was ever to get to the bottom of the mystery surrounding my brother's disappearance, I would have to go far more deeply into these whispered tales of vague forms seen on High Tor, hideous noises that tore the black, moonless nights asunder and woke half of the village with their bloodcurdling shrieks, and even go up to that accursed place of black stone columns and graven ideographs far above the village.

The weather did not improve any

during the day and night came early to Tor mount. After supper, I went up to the room that Lindennan had prepared for me. It was situated at one corner of the house so that I might look out both upon the sea and the rearing hills behind where they stretched black and ominous against the misty sky, curving around the wide bay, out to the spot where the ruined column of Dark Point lighthouse stood atop its out-thrusting promontory.

There were, I noticed, several small fishing vessels out in the bay, but without exception, all of them remained well clear of the spot where the lighthouse and the ruined village lay and I knew by some strange instinct that this was not only because of dangerous shoals and reefs in that area. The sound of the incoming tide was now very insistent and I found my gaze drawn irresistibly towards the lighthouse. It occurred to me that perhaps there was some natural explanation for all of these whispered tales, some lingering memory of that cataclysmic happening when an entire village had been destroyed. Witchcraft had been rife in those days throughout the whole of England, but nowhere had it been so deeply rooted as here. Superstition would die hard and slowly here and what more natural than that, over the centuries, these tales would be grossly exaggerated, handed down by word of mouth in this tightly-knit and isolated community of simple-minded people?

Yet Lindennan was an intelligent and cultured man, and he plainly believed them. Terrible and mad deeds had been perpetrated in those far-distant years, tainting these people with their touch of evil. I resolved to try to find that apocryphal book of peculiar characters of which my host had spoken, a book which he claimed might tell the true meaning behind these things, might throw some light on Philip's disappearance, for it came to me that perhaps, by some ill-gotten chance, he may have discovered it and found the means of interpreting those forgotten symbols, might have learned far too much from it.

One thing was certain — I would have to stay in Tor Mount for some time, for although my desire to discover what had happened to my brother had faded a little in my fear and loathing, I knew I would never rest easily again unless I did. The thought came to me that there might be a germ of truth in the legends, that some sea-spawned monstrosity had come up from the deeps in those far-off days, some gigantic squid perhaps, and left an indelible impression on these fisherfolk, haunting their dreams, colouring their lives and actions. But even if this were so, inconceivable as it might seem, the actuality must have died almost four centuries before, explaining perhaps, those strange bones which Lindennan and the others had found in the crumbling lighthouse.

The riot of ideas that formed chaotically in my mind brought a mounting unrest and despite the deep weariness in my body, sleep seemed as far off as ever. I tried to give my thoughts as neutral and composed a cast as possible as I watched the twilight deepen over those barren, curiously-shaped hills that flanked the shoreline behind the village. Their contours were softened by the writhing mist, but not in any way that brought beauty to them; rather, the fog tended to enhance the air of brooding malignancy that lay over them. At times, it was just possible for me to make out the symmetrical stone pillars on top of the highest peak, which I took to be High Tor. Watching them as darkness fell, I thought over what Lindennan had told me of those witchcraft rites and conclaves, which had been held there in days gone by and the outward connection between that circle of carven stones and the ruined village of Torsands. The similarity between what had happened here and the destruction of Sodom and Gomorrah was obvious and may have provided a basis for those legends.

For a long while, I did not undress but sat by the wide window, struggling to analyse my thoughts only to find to my intense uneasiness that I seemed to be subconsciously waiting for something to happen — my ears straining to pick out some sound which I dreaded to hear but to which I could put no name. There was no doubt that my host's colourful story had worked far more deeply and intensely on my imagination than I had previously imagined.

At length, feeling a physical fatigue brought about by the long journey of the previous night, I half undressed and lay down on the bed, closing my eyes in an attempt to sleep, but the mental drowsiness was a long time in coming, and when I finally did fall into a fitful doze, it was to be haunted by intermittent dreams into which the most frightful sounds seemed to penetrate. On one occasion, I seemed to awaken from my sleep, startled by a loud crash that originated from somewhere outside the room. I must have been half-awake for I sat bolt upright on my bed, my entire body palpitating uncontrollably. There was a faint glow of moonlight showing through the windows and from where I sat it was just possible for me to make out the headland with High Tor rising to one side. I braced myself tensely in expectation of some fearful and imponderable menace which seemed to be pressing itself close around the house, emanating from the hills and the sea and then, without warning, there came those deep-pitched roaring overtones of sound which must have been the cause of my awakening and which will never leave my mind to my last day. It was almost wrong to call them sounds because to my sleep-drugged mind the noises seemed to be shaping themselves into *words*. The ghastly infra-bass timbre boomed and roared as if some tremendous struggle was going on and then, incredibly, shockingly, freezing the blood in my veins, there came that stuttering, shuddering, final frenzy of noise:

'Hyaaaaaayaaa . . . Hyaaa . . . Help! Help me! Bill! BILL!'

From what terrible abyss those sounds emanated, I had no way of telling, and the fact that whatever it was had called my name, in a voice which, in spite of those thunderous and oddly alien overtones, seemed oddly like Philip's, made me shake convulsively on the bed, fingers clenching spasmodically by my sides.

I have said that I was uncertain

whether or not I was really awake. Even at that moment, I could not be sure, for this was surely something bred more out of nightmare than wakefulness. Certainly the experience transcended anything I had ever known. Later, once those harsh croaking sounds had died away I must have fallen asleep again, but the ephemeral memory of what I thought I had heard entered and tinged my dreams so that my sleeping mind clawed and scratched through shuddering nightmares in which pulsing madness and inconceivable vistas stretched before my inner vision and I saw vague, formless shadows stalk out of fathomless chasms of nighted rock.

In the morning, with the sun shining brilliantly over the sea, glinting off the incoming waves and the rocky hills glowing purple and green on the landward skyline, I intimated my intentions to Lindennan, who warned me bravely against probing too deeply into such things, at least before I knew the sort of thing I was up against. When he saw that I was determined to go through with it, he hinted that perhaps Ben Trevelyan might be able to tell me things I wanted to know, that in any case, he was the only other person in the village who would talk, if only I could get him into the right frame of mind. He was a strange, furtive character, a little simple in the head, and no one could be sure how much truth there was in his crazy ramblings.

Judging from Lindennan's opinion of Trevelyan, I doubted if any useful information could be gained from him but at that point I knew I could not afford to pass over a single clue, and half an hour later I made my way along the narrow street which fronted the row of decrepit houses, crossing a swift-running stream, which ran down from the hills, passing several of the boats which were drawn up along the shore where the smooth sand gave way to a narrow fringe of shingle. There were men working with the nets but none of them looked up as I approached, keeping their gaze downcast, although where I had passed them, I knew they were watching my retreating back closely. Some of the houses were obviously tenanted, but I caught no glimpse of anyone in them and the curtainless, broken windows of the others, looking out towards the distant sea possessed a frightening aspect, so much so that it took courage to walk past them towards a short row of three tumbledown cottages, in one of which Ben Trevelyan was reputed to live.

I had approached within fifty yards of the cottages when I caught sight of the bent figure seated on a low stoop beside the centre cottage. One glance was sufficient to tell me that this could be none other than the half-crazed, oldest inhabitant — Ben Trevelyan.

Pushing open the creaking gate that swung in on rusty hinges, I went into the overgrown garden that looked as though it had seen better days, but not for many years, and stood in front of the other for several seconds before he gave any indication that he was aware of my presence. Then he gave me a quick, shrewd glance and I noticed, to my surprise there was a bright gleam of intelligence in his rheumy eyes that surveyed me intently from head to toe.

Giving me a knowing leer, he bent forward, motioned me towards the seat and hissed sibilantly: 'Reckon I know why you're here, mister. Come about them happenings at Dark Point, ain't you?'

'I'm trying to find out what happened to my brother, Philip Meredith.'

He nodded abruptly, tilted his head forward confidentially: 'There's things I know you'd never believe. Up yonder is where it all started on High Tor.' He lifted a shaking arm and pointed to the rounded summit that brooded evilly in the sunlight. 'Used to hold ceremonies up there long ago. More'n four hundred years ago, they reckon. Brought the Devil up out of the sea. Called Him up into Dark Point lighthouse. Fixed up a place for Him there so He'd bring 'em all the fish they wanted out in the bay. They learnt many things in them days. How to bring down the thunder and lightning. How to start the rain when there be a drought. But there was a price they had to pay.'

He stretched out a bony finger, tapped

me on the knee, his face close to mine. There was a terrible insistence in his voice that brought a shiver coursing through my body. Listening to him, it was becoming more and more difficult not to believe some of the things he uttered, incredible and utterly fantastic as they sounded.

'Every May Eve, they'd have human sacrifices up there on High Tor, just to keep things right for another year and there'd be chantin' and shriekin' and dancin' all night and pretty soon, things got so heathen and devilish that nobody from the other towns and villages would come anywhere near the place. Reckon they must've gone a bit too far one time and called down the wrath of God Himself on 'em because one night a great wave came up out of the sea and drowned 'em all, every last one of 'em. But that didn't stop things. S'long as that light stands on Dark Point, things'll still go on like in the old times, only they keep it all hidden now. But I've seen and heard things up yonder on the hill and in Dark Point lighthouse — and I do know where

Winters and Sloane and Marcy went; and maybe all 'em others who went out to take a look around yon accursed place. How'd you like to crouch on the sand and watch that horrible *transfiguration* take place, see men go into the lighthouse and things come out that weren't even like anythin' you'd ever seen afore in your whole life? Just how it was done, Heaven only knows; or maybe Heaven just doesn't want to know because it was more like the Devil's work. These abominations came from somewhere out of time and space as we know it. They were here before men were and they'll be here long after we've all gone.'

He stopped at that and his eyes clouded as thoughts crowded in and it was as though the memories evoked by his words were more than his aged mind could stand. Then he began to laugh shrilly, lips shaking behind the unkempt grey beard.

'Reckon you're beginnin' to see now, ain't ye? Guessed you might. But that ain't all.' He held a taloned hand on my sleeve, fingers biting in with an incredible strength. His eyes blinked rapidly as he went on: 'You don't have to believe just because I say so. It's all written down in a book the old ones left behind, only nobody can read it. Ain't like no language I ever seen. Had a professor down at the end of the last century. Came from Oxford or someplace like that. Wanted to take it away with him but they wouldn't let him. In the end, he said it was nothin' more than a lot of symbols that didn't mean anything.' He shivered as he spoke, tightened his grip on my arm. 'But there's a meanin' all right, if only you can read it. I tried but it was no use. Funny sort o' language, all straight lines and — ' He broke off sharply, his eyelids twitching as he stared past me, past the village, up to where the dark column of the shuttered lighthouse stood illuminated by the sun. For a long moment, he said nothing more, then he heaved himself to his feet, moved back towards the house.

'I ain't said nothin' for a very long time now. Too many of those who tried to find out went the way of Sloane and the others, up to that damned place.' He leaned forward for a second, hissed through stained and broken teeth: 'You know where real horror is? You know what'll happen if I want to show you that book? It ain't so much what's up there on High Tor now. But if you wants to know what happened to Philip Meredith — you say he was your brother — then I reckon you'll have to meet the Keeper of Dark Point. Ain't no other way I can see, even though you'll probably go the same way as the rest.'

He led the way into the cottage and almost before I could collect my scattered wits had rummaged through a pile of dusty books in one corner of the room, bringing one of them back to me and placing it, almost reverently, into my hands. It was plainly of great age, the mildewed leather cover stained in places as if by salt water, testifying to its authenticity. For a moment I could scarcely dare to open it. When I did so, I found that the pages were covered with the faded writing about which I had heard so much. The symbols and diagrams were sufficient to evoke a shuddering revulsion; a clutching, pervasive fear in me that was terribly difficult to overcome.

In answer to my insistent requests to be allowed to keep the book for a few days in order that I might attempt to decipher the weird ideographs, some of which bore a frightening resemblance to certain letters and phrases I had seen before in writing that is kept under lock and key at the British Museum, especially one or two paragraphs in the infamous *Necronomicon,* Trevelyan grudgingly agreed although it was clear from the expression on his face that he considered me both impetuous and foolish in the extreme to dabble in these hidden mysteries.

It still being only ten-thirty, I decided to climb the narrow winding path that led up the side of High Tor in order that I might examine that rough circle of stone pillars by daylight. As I climbed, I discovered traces of an old road, mostly obliterated among huge tangled growths and abnormally stunted trees but showing here and there as a greyish scar in the undergrowth. Here was all of the primal mystery of Earth's beginnings and I knew, by some strange instinct, that this place was unutterably vile and evil. Too many deep shadows were there for my liking and there was not one solitary rustle of a creature in that matted undergrowth, not a single bird singing on the branches of any of the trees.

I came upon the crude circle of stones on the brow of the hill where the ground was level and even the corrupt growth seemed to shun this place for here was merely an open stretch of flat grey rock, totally devoid of any vegetation, with those tall pillars set around a wide, flat stone in the very centre of the circle. I went closer, scarcely able to repress a shudder of nauseous revulsion, a sense of alarm at the knowledge that this was not the Roman site as I had first thought, nor a Celtic temple. This was something far older and far more terrifying in its implications than anything I could have imagined, for the carvings on the weathered stone were similar in outline to those on Easter Island, but more awful — and there was something curious about the weathering of the storm as if these pillars had, at some time in their past incredible history, been under the sea. I found myself shuddering at what this so clearly implied and at the terrible portentousness of those hideous carvings, many of which were like symbols in the book, which had been lent to me by the half-crazed Ben Trevelyan.

But the greatest horror was that flat stone slab of smooth, carved rock in the centre of the ring. There did seem to be some time-effaced marks around the base of it; but on the top, the unmistakable discolouration where the blood of God alone knew how many hapless victims had soaked into the stone. I could no longer doubt the veracity of some of Trevelyan's odd tale and even though my mind rejected the idea that these things can still be happening in this day and age, I could not prevent myself from glancing nervously over my shoulder every few moments. If only there had been some sound up there on that hilltop, some birdsong, the rustle of some tiny creature among those grossly abnormal growths.

The stillness ate at my nerves like acid. Every sense screamed at me to get away from that unhallowed spot. An acute terror rose into my mind now and clutching the leather-bound volume I turned and fled down the hillside, oblivious to the thorns which scratched my flesh and strove to impede my progress.

That afternoon, I made my first attempt to decipher the cryptic writing in the ancient volume. I hardly need say that I struggled ineffectually for several hours, making use of such books as Lindennan possessed — for it turned out that he, too, like my brother, had long been interested in these matters, had once seen the book I now had and tried to read it himself, but without any success. The more deeply, I delved into it, the more certain I became that without the aid of the *Necronomicon,* it would be utterly impossible to make any sense at all of the cryptic writing. There were, it is true, certain irregularities about the symbols, which suggested a highly developed form of language, but it was clearly one that pre-dated even the ancient Sumerian, which I knew quite well. I made exhaustive attempts to determine the form of the language, trying several of the old scripts, including the ancient hieroglyphics of Egypt and the Aztec symbolism, but to no avail.

For the next two days, Lindennan and I discussed the matter, poring over the tattered pages of the volume until well into the night. What outlandish hand had written the original material I could only guess at. Certainly it did not seem to have belonged to Earth, of that I felt sure. Of course, it might all have been one gigantic fraud and if I had been handed the volume anywhere else and under any other circumstances, I would have been more ready to believe such information. But too many things had happened at Tor Mount for me to even consider such an idea.

It was not until late on the third evening of my stay there that we obtained our first clue, one that enabled me to translate much of what was written there. The hieroglyphics were in the dark and dreaded Aklo language used by the ancient and evil cults at the beginning of man's sojourn on this planet, lost for centuries following the decline and fall of Lemuria. While my host slept that night, I sat in my room, painstakingly going through the strange volume, finding myself faced with names I had heard at times from my brother, associated with the most hideous connections, and whose significance was to become so terrifying for me; for as dawn was greying the heavens over the ghostly finger of Dark Point, I knew the dark and dreadful secret which lay at the back of the myths and legends of terror-haunted Tor Mount, knew the meaning of those black stones on High Tor and what Trevelyan, in his demented ravings had meant by the Keeper of Dark Point!

* * *

Shortly before ten the next evening, despite Lindennan's warning and earnest entreaties, I left the isolated cottage and made my way along the sands towards

Dark Point. For what I had succeeded in reading in that awful tome made it imperative I should go there, made it impossible for me to do anything else but meet the dreaded Keeper of Dark Point face-to-face.

It was dark by the time I had crossed the stretch of sandy beach and stood at the base of the promontory on which the lighthouse stood, rearing its decaying column of stone towards the evil stars, and the moon was just rising from the horizon out to sea, throwing a pale, ghostly luminescence across the silently heaving water. There was no doubting that the stone walls of the tower were in a state of great decrepitude and many of the blocks of masonry of which it had been constructed had fallen and lay around it in great, shadow-strewn heaps. The main doorway was closed with strips of stone, wood nailed across it, refusing the entry and adding to the sense of sinister malevolence that hung like an invisible shroud over the place.

I knew — or at least I thought I knew — what I would find in this evil structure, yet the tremendously terrible lure held me fast, forcing my dragging feet forward, around the massive base until I came upon the shattered opening to the rear by which the party of men from Tor Mount had gained entrance when they had come looking for my brother. God! If only they had known what I knew then! If only they knew how fiendishly close they had been to such nightmare terror as the mind of man could scarcely comprehend.

Moving almost without conscious volition, I crept inside, shuffling over the dust-covered floor. There was one dark corner in which I made out the shape of the stone stairs that wound around the inside of the tower, leading up to the very top where the light had once been. Keeping my feelings in check with the greatest difficulty, I climbed the stairs to the next floor, stood in the dimness, bracing myself, before switching on my electric torch and playing the beam around the room. There was an oppressive, stifling atmosphere there, which caught up my throat and froze the breath in my lungs.

In that eldritch place, I saw those nightmare things exactly as Lindennan had described to me; the irregularly-shaped stone plinth the centre of the room and behind those warped and twisted bones, yellowing with age and curiously shaped. The mere sight of some of them twisted the muscles of my stomach into a hard, jangled knot.

I spent little time there but continued up those winding stairs. In places the stone blocks had fallen, leaving wide gaps across which I was forced to jump. At length, I reached the top of the stairs. Above me, set high in the ceiling, with a short flight of steps leading up to it, this time from the centre of the chamber, was set the trapdoor that Lindennan had mentioned. But unlike those men who had preceded me, I had one piece of dread knowledge which they had not possessed; one which, if they had known, would have sent them screaming from that place of terror and ancient, eldritch things.

Stillness pressed down on me from all sides, yet I was acutely conscious of something close by, formless perhaps, but eyeing me with a horrible intensity. For a fleeting moment, I wondered what had happened to those men — and those other *alien* creatures — whose bodies lay on that dusty floor beneath me. Then, all thought of that fled my mind. The silence was broken by a sound that came from directly above me, from just beyond that closed trapdoor.

The hideous shuffling and inhuman slopping almost made me faint on the spot. It seemed, in my state of overwrought fear and imagination, that the boards of the ceiling over my head bent and swayed as though a monstrous weight was heaving itself in the direction of the trapdoor. After a moment, there came a further sound, the rattling of an iron bolt that held the door in place. The muffled creaking of the floor continued. And then there came the greatest of terrors. It would be almost impossible to describe the noises that issued from that dreadful room above me. A frightful baying and roaring, which began softly and rose swiftly in volume until the sound shrieked in my ears. It was the same sound that had woken me on my first night in the cottage half a mile or so away, but now there was that voice in it, the hoarse barking and hesitantly-syllabled croaking which resembled speech, as though an animal were trying to imitate a human voice; yet it was no human throat that was making those roaring, sibilant utterings.

Would to God that I had turned and fled precipitously at the first intimation of danger. The sounds were nothing more nor less than an awful echo of those malignant, accursed mumblings of elder evil that have sounded down unimaginable ages and across terrible abysses of outer hells from the beginning of time. Eternities seemed to elapse as I stood fixed to the spot, unable to move my limbs. Then, slowly, the trapdoor began to lift. A tiny rim of utter blackness showed, widening with every succeeding sound. A wave of sheer terror swept over me. A nauseous fishy odour seeped down from that midnight-black opening and engulfed me, and as I watched, the beam from my torch, playing over the aperture — my throat choked by that clammy stench of rottenness and decay — I found myself face-to-face with that dreadful Keeper of Dark Point.

From what black abyss of hellish fear, from what terrible gulf of cosmic and grotesque horror that thing had been drawn, I could not even begin to guess. Monstrous in outline, it remained poised in that dark opening, muttering that weird whistling roar which froze the blood in my veins and forced my brain to the edge of screaming madness. It seemed partly human with the head of a man, wide eyes staring down unblinkingly at the light from the torch, but there all resemblance ended. I caught a fragmentary glimpse of waving tentacles or feelers, blood-red suckers at the ends, which reached down from the opening towards me. The mere sight of the thing crowded out all other thoughts from my mind. I must have lost consciousness for a second. The next thing I remember stumbling down the twisting stairs, falling and picking myself up as I got to the bottom, pursued by that dreadful whistling, by that fearful blast of sound that echoed and re-echoed throughout the crumbling tower. There was a nightmare flight across the sand with the sea booming against the rocks and the evil, pallid moonlight, throwing grotesque shadows over everything.

As I ran, I thought of all I had succeeded in reading in the strange book, all of the dread secrets I had, in my ignorance, unlocked. I knew now the meaning behind those terrible and puzzling prints that had been found in the sand that day after my brother had vanished from Dark Point lighthouse and I could guess at the horror that those simple folk had dredged up from the vast deeps by their chants and sacrifices on the top of High Tor. Had they but known what sort of horror they were unleashing, they might have thought twice about what they were doing, might have left things as they were. God alone knows how many poor devils were lured into that blasphemous place and once there, fell under the irresistible spell of the Keeper. For a single blinding flash of clarity — or perhaps, although all reason was virtually gone before the sight of that hideous creature — I saw everything as it must really have been. The terrible, outwordly transformations which must have taken place in that room at the top of the tower, the black thing of the elder voids which could not return to the Deep unless it could develop and transform in some ghastly transmigration of identity with a human sufficiently foolish as to wander into that place and come face-to-face with it.

Before that night, I would never have been able to accept an explanation such as this. Now, after what I had seen, I know there are unguessed and untold horrors, which exist just beyond the edge of reason and life, lurking on the very rim of things until man's prying brings them forth to slaver and destroy.

That thing which had gone back into the sea with my brother; that hideous entity which had made those shocking prints in the sand beside his — it had become fully changed, making its way back to the sea, back to the abysmal depths which lay out beyond the reefs offshore. What those men had overlooked when they had searched the area the next morning was that there were also prints leading up *out* of the sea, going *back* into Dark Point lighthouse — the prints of the thing which my brother had become — half-changed; forced to wait until someone, more curious than the rest, went there alone and waited for that trapdoor to open, waited petrified for sight of that half-creature of the Deeps.

I could have told the police what I saw, but they would not have believed. Ben Trevelyan knows, but his wild, demented ravings are, of course, ignored, and as for Lindennan, although he half-believes, he is content to leave these black nameless things alone. What he will do, very soon, when I go back to Dark Point lighthouse for the last time, I do not know. Perhaps then, he will tell them all he knows and try to make them believe, force them to take dynamite and destroy that accursed place once and for all.

For I shall go back, I *must* go back.

There is now no way by which I can prevent myself. I am writing this in the hope that someone may read and believe all that has happened. Even though that last, final horror may have turned my brain so that I can no longer really say that what happened is the truth and not a nightmare; for crazed though I undoubtedly was — *the face of that black horror which looked down at me from that open trapdoor was that of Philip Meredith — my brother!*

THE END

Other titles in the
Linford Mystery Library:

DEADLY MEMOIR

Ardath Mayhar

When Margaret Thackrey, ex-government agent and writer, decides to pen her memoirs, she unwittingly gets the attention of a vicious assassin — a man whose nefarious deeds she'd nearly uncovered during her service. Now he must stop the publication of her book before his true character is revealed. He murders Margaret's husband, and stalks her from Oregon to Texas, where she must finally confront her past — and a determined, stone-cold killer!

THE GRAB

Gordon Landsborough

In Istanbul, a beautiful girl is grabbed from her hotel bed and taken out into the night. But Professional Trouble-Buster Joe P. Heggy is looking on and decides to investigate: who was the girl and why was she kidnapped? But when thugs try to eliminate him, he is equal to their attempts, especially when he's aided by a bunch of American construction workers. Then things get very tense when Heggy finds the girl — and then kidnaps her himself . . .